THE GASLIGHT STALKER

Esther & Jack Enright Mystery
Book One

David Field

SAPERE
BOOKS

THE GASLIGHT STALKER

Published by Sapere Books.

11 Bank Chambers, Hornsey, London, N8 7NN,
United Kingdom

saperebooks.com

ISBN: 978-1-912546-03-9

Chapter One

It was the Monday evening of the August Bank Holiday weekend of 1888, and most of the noisy crowd in the White Hart public bar on Whitechapel's High Street had been drinking all day.

'Mucky Meg' Drinkwater was insisting on singing another ditty, stout glass in one hand and nose warmer pipe in the other, and landlord Jack Brougham warned her that if it was as filthy as the last one, she'd be out on her ear. Meg barely made it into the second verse before Jack grabbed her by the neck of her tight bodice and dragged her to the open doorway, throwing her bodily into the street amid the outraged shouts of protests from his male customers, many of whom appeared to be off-duty Coldstream Guardsmen from Wellington Barracks, who'd spent the day slumming.

Esther Jacobs narrowly missed being bowled over as she approached the doorway in time to see Meg skid along the cobbles, skirt up and boots flailing in the warm evening air. Esther took a deep breath and persevered, craning her neck through the thick smoke for a sight of her friend, Martha Turner, who she'd come to find. Eventually she spied her, propping up the bar counter, although knowing Martha the bar counter was probably keeping her upright. Esther pushed and dodged her way through the motley crowd of soldiers, labourers, ne'er-do-wells and their whores for the evening, apologising here and there as she was obliged to employ a bony elbow on her way through. As she reached Martha's side, her friend gave her a stupid grin of recognition and threw her arm across Esther's shoulder.

''Ello there, lovey — care ter join me in a small refreshment, would yer?'

'I'm only here with a message,' Esther insisted. 'Harry's back, and he's asking for you.'

Martha's face fell as she took another swig of her beer. 'Did 'e say anythin' about money?'

'No, he just sent me to find you. This is the third pub I've been in.'

'I always drinks in the White 'Art, yer knows that. I hopes yer 'aven't bin inconvenienced on my account?'

'I had to come out for candles anyway,' Esther reassured her. 'The Superintendent's turned the gas off again and I have some work to finish. On the way out I bumped into Harry and he asked me to keep a lookout for you.'

Martha spat into the sawdust.

''E's after 'is money, that's all. Either that, or a bit of 'owzyerfarver. Either way, I'm stayin' where I am, thank yer very much.'

'He's your husband, Martha,' Esther reminded her, 'and your place is with him, not these dreadful louts in here.'

'If I go 'ome now, wi' a few drinks under me stays, 'e'll belt the shit outa me, like 'e normally does when I bin on the razzle-dazzle. An' I owes 'im a couple o' bob from the last time I saw 'im, up by Aldgate pump. I were meant ter get stock fer the business, but as yer can see, I found a better use fer it. Care ter join me?'

'No thanks.' Esther grimaced as she watched another fight break out in the corner from which Meg had recently been removed. Tables, chairs and glasses went in all directions and Jack Brougham waded in with two of his fixers to restore order.

'Right enough, it's gettin' a bit lively in 'ere,' Martha conceded. 'What say we move inter the snug? What's yer poison these days?'

'I don't drink, as you know,' Esther reminded her, 'but I'll have a small glass of mild, if — and only if, mind you — you make it your last, then come home to Harry.'

'We'll get the drinks from Jack then take 'em through wi' us,' Martha suggested. 'They charges more in the snug, though God alone knows they charges enough in 'ere. 'Alf o' mild, weren't it?'

'Yes please,' Esther confirmed, then frowned as she saw that Martha had ordered her a pint instead. They weaved their way towards the side door and moved through it into the more sedate snug bar. As they did so, Martha cursed quietly and grabbed Esther by the elbow, nearly spilling her drink in the process.

'Over 'ere,' Martha hissed. 'This table by the door. There's somebody over there I don't want ter see right now. I'll sit wi' me back to 'er, facin' the door, an' you can take the seat across from me.'

As they settled at the table, Esther was curious. 'Who is it you want to avoid?' she enquired.

Martha snorted as she mixed her own 'dog's nose' by pouring the double measure of gin into her beer glass and took a deep draught, wiping the froth from her mouth as she replied: 'Her, over in the corner, wi' three other totties. She's the big fat 'un wi' an 'at full o' dead crows an' a face like a busted arse.'

Esther looked across the small room and seated in the far corner, attended by three women whose gaudy attire, overdone face makeup and gay bonnets loudly announced their profession, was a much larger and older woman, dressed all in black, with a monstrous headpiece covered in feathers and a masculine face that did not bode well for her prospects if she intended to compete with her companions for the business of the soldiers who were clearly only here for one thing.

They sat at an adjoining table.

'Who is she?' Esther enquired.

'They calls 'er Pearly Poll. Fucked if I knows 'er proper name, but that's the name she goes by. Nasty piece o' work an' I owes 'er money an' all.'

Esther sighed. 'Is there anyone you don't owe money to?'

'None o' yourn. But Pearly Poll's not the sort o' woman yer wants ter be obliged to.'

'Does she employ bully boys to collect her debts?' Esther enquired, concerned for her friend's safety.

Another snort from Martha. 'She don't need ter. She can whack 'em 'arder than most blokes. Look at the size of 'er, fer Christ's sake. She was the biggest tottie in Whitechapel in 'er day, so they reckons. Nowadays she just lives off what she can get by runnin' other girls, like the ones what's sittin' wi' er over at the table.'

'How do you know all this?' Esther asked, although she thought she already knew the answer.

'I used ter do a bit o' tottin' meself, years back, but I give it up after one o' them gimme three busted ribs. That's afore I met 'Arry, o' course, an' I wouldn't go back ter that way o' livin' if me life depended on it. It's a rough enough life street tradin', God knows, but it's better than tottin', an' I finished wi' all that years ago.'

'Don't look now, but she's coming over here,' Esther warned Martha, who muttered 'fuck' and ducked her head down.

Poll smacked Martha on the back of the head, at the same time smiling down at Esther. 'It's bin six weeks, arse'ole —

where's me fuckin' five bob?' Poll demanded as she took the vacant seat.

Martha cringed and looked up. 'Next week, I promise yer — 'onest. It's just that we've 'ad ter get more stock in an' until we gets ter sell it ...'

'Don't gimme that shit! The whole o' Whitechapel knows that 'Arry left yer weeks since an' yet yer got plenty o' money fer grog, by the looks o' things.'

'It's the truth, honest ter God!' Martha protested. It fell silent for a moment as Poll looked Esther up and down in a manner that made the young girl feel uncomfortable.

'Well now,' Poll said eventually, 'there's several ways we might come ter some arrangement regardin' the money yer owes me. As yer can see, me friends an' I are gettin' some attention from them sojer boys at the next table. There's five o' them an' only four of us, so why don't yer earn yerself a pretty shillin' on yer back? Or mebbe yer friend 'ere instead? She's gotta be worth twice that, even standin' up, what wi' 'er bein' so fresh and pretty an' all. Waddyer say, girl?' she enquired with a suggestive leer at Esther.

'She ain't goin' tottin' fer you an' that's a certainty,' Martha insisted while Esther recovered from the shock. 'She's a respectable young lady an' she's my friend, so leave 'er out've it.'

'Pity,' Poll replied as she looked Esther up and down again with an experienced eye. 'If yer prefer, she can come 'ome wi me an' I'll find 'er some way o' payin' yer debt off, depend on it.'

Esther hastily swallowed the last of her drink and stood up. 'We have to be going now, I'm afraid. Martha's husband's waiting for her at home and I have to get back to work.'

'What sorta work d'yer do at this time on a public 'oliday?' Poll demanded.

'I'm a seamstress,' Esther advised her, 'and I work from home.'

Polly looked more closely at her flowing black curls, aquiline nose and smooth thin lips. 'You a Yid?'

'I'm Jewish, certainly.'

'Where d'ya live?'

'Spitalfields — up the road there. In the same house as my friend Martha here. And we need to be going now.'

'I'll stay 'ere a while longer, if it's all the same ter you,' Martha replied quietly. 'Tell 'Arry I'll be 'ome soon.'

'You're not going back on the game I hope?' Esther demanded.

Martha shook her head. 'Like I said, them days is over fer me. But I can mebbe sort out some sort've arrangement with Poll 'ere, which yer mebbe shouldn't be knowin' about. So just you pop off 'ome an' tell 'Arry I'm not long be'ind yer.'

Esther walked sadly back out through the public bar, shaking her head and wondering how she was going to explain things to Harry when she got home. The bar was slightly less crowded than it had been, but she was obliged to step carefully around several piles of vomit and an insensible drunk as she made her way into the street, turning left into Osbourne Street until it became Brick Lane, then into Thrawl Street. There she stopped off briefly at the chandler's shop that never seemed to close and purchased four candles and a box of matches. Then it was a right turn into George Street, towards Satchell's Lodging House at number 19.

As she passed the alleyway that led up to the glue factory she heard a bestial grunting noise and peered into the shadows, where a woman was bent double, her skirts hitched to her waist. A man was ramming into her from behind with determination and obvious satisfaction. Esther's stomach turned and she walked quickly on, reaching the safety of the side alley entrance to the rooming house that she'd called home for the past year or so.

Harry Turner came out of the ground floor common kitchen as he heard the sound of her approaching boots in the entrance hall and stood directly in front of her, barring her passage.

'Well? Did yer find 'er?'

'I did and she's in the White Hart, with an old acquaintance of hers.'

'An' who might that be?'

'I think her name was Polly, or something like that.'

'Pearly fuckin' Poll? Was that 'er?'

'Could have been,' Esther admitted, her eyes on the floor.

'Fuckin' whore!' Harry yelled, as the colour rose rapidly in his face. 'She's back ter the tottin' again, ain't she? An' her a respectable married woman what's got a man waitin' at 'ome while she goes openin' 'er fat legs ter some drunken cock. When she gets 'ome, tell 'er from me that we're finally finished this time. I don't want a dose o' the fuckin' pox next time she looks in my direction. You tell 'er that from me, understood?'

'Yes, Harry,' Esther replied meekly, fearful that he might strike her in his rage. Then as he stormed out through the side entrance Esther walked up the two flights of stairs to her own room on the second floor, glancing sadly at the closed door of the room across the landing that in better days was home to Martha and Harry Turner. They had befriended her when circumstances had forced her to take cheap lodgings in a single room that overlooked the catsmeat yard that George and Sadie Thompson operated from the ground floor rear flat, while George supplemented their business with his meagre wage as

Superintendent of the common lodging house that the Satchells owned — one of many cheap doss houses that they maintained in the Spitalfields district.

Spitalfields had been Esther's only home for her twenty-three years in life. First the three-storied house in White Lion Street, the ground floor of which had been her parents' fabric import warehouse until, when Esther was only seventeen, they had both been killed when the Sunday afternoon Thames pleasure boat they had been passengers on capsized as it was turning against a heavy incoming tide at Woolwich. This had made orphans of Esther and her older brother Abe, who'd joined the army almost immediately afterwards, leaving Esther to fend for herself.

Fortunately for her, the Jacobs family had enjoyed both a lengthy business relationship and a family link with Isaac and Ruth Rosen, who took Esther in and taught her all she knew about garment manufacture and repair from their premises in Lamb Street, where Esther had occupied the top garret and enjoyed three hearty meals a day in exchange for her proven skills with both needle and sewing machine. Then came the anti-Semitic riot almost a year ago that had led to the burning down of the Rosens' garment factory, from which Esther had barely escaped with her life, clad only in her nightgown. She'd been forced to find somewhere else to live, but fortunately the Rosens had not given up and Esther made a living of sorts performing 'outwork' for them as they slowly rebuilt their business.

She'd been living a solitary life on the top floor of Satchells, keeping herself to herself, when Martha and Harry moved in across the landing and she and Martha had developed a friendship in the communal ground floor kitchen. Esther knew that Harry occasionally beat Martha and that he had a foul temper even when sober, which was most of the time. She could hear them at it even across the landing and she would curl up on her bed, block her ears and pray for Martha's safety until it was over. Martha would appear the next morning, her plump face covered in bruises, but still smiling and Esther could only admire her courage, wondering at the same time why she put up with it. But in her lonelier moments, Esther told herself that even a husband who beat you around the face occasionally was probably a better prospect than no husband at all on a permanent basis. One day, perhaps, she mused as the trousers she was taking in slipped from her knees when she nodded off in her chair beside the truckle bed.

She awoke the next morning with stiff muscles to the sound of heavy banging on her door. Sleepily, she walked the few feet across her room and opened it, coming face to face with a red-faced Harry Turner, tears streaming down his cheeks. He was obviously not in the mood for idle chit-chat as he grabbed her by the collar of her jacket and dragged her into the hallway, demanding that she go with him down to the kitchen.

'Why?' she gasped.

''Cos there's a Peeler down there an' he wants ter talk ter yer about Martha.'

Down in the kitchen, a nervous and absurdly young-looking police constable stood waiting for her by the sink, notebook at the ready. 'Miss Jacobs?' he enquired.

'That's me,' she acknowledged. 'What's this about?'

'I'm Constable Barrett, H Division, Leman Street. I'm informed that you were with your friend Martha yesterday evening in the White Hart public house in Whitechapel High Street.'

'That's correct.'

'Did you leave her there?'

'Yes.'

'About what time?'

'It must have been around eleven. Why, what's she done?'

'She's done nothing, miss. It's what's been done to her.'

'I beg your pardon?'

'Someone's done her in on the stairwell of George Yard Buildings and you were the last person we know of who saw her alive.'

Chapter Two

Esther was still in the same state of shocked disbelief two days later, as she sat to the side of the main body of spectators inside the Working Lads' Institute in Whitechapel Road, listening to Deputy Coroner George Collier formally opening the inquest into the death of 'a woman unknown, believed at this stage to be one Martha Turner, of 19 George Street, Spitalfields'. Esther had been asked to sit to one side by the senior police officer, Detective Inspector Reid, who had advised her that this is where the witnesses called to the inquest would sit until they had given their testimony. She felt very self-conscious of all the eyes upon her, particularly those of Pearly Poll, who sat near the back of the hall, glaring at her, alongside another woman of about the same age whose face looked familiar to Esther as one of those who had been at the table with Poll in the snug bar on the last occasion that Esther had seen her friend Martha.

She was still wondering what on earth she could add to the proceedings when the first witness was called. He was the young police constable who had broken the terrible news to Esther in the kitchen of her lodgings two days ago and after taking the oath, being asked to read from his notebook, and clearing his throat rather pompously, he began: 'I am Police Constable Thomas Barrett, H172, Metropolitan Police, stationed at Leman Street Police Office. At approximately 5 am on 7th August past, I was proceeding along my beat in the general vicinity of Whitechapel High Street when I was approached by a Mr. John Reeves, who advised me that he had discovered the body of a woman, believed dead, in the stairwell of George Yard Buildings, a common lodging house.

'I proceeded to said stairwell, where I located the body of the deceased, lying on her back in a pool of blood. She was wearing a black bonnet, a long black jacket, a dark green skirt and stockings. Her lower clothing had been raised to waist height and she appeared to be deceased. I remained with the body and directed the witness Reeves to summon Dr Killeen, who arrived at approximately five thirty am and pronounced the victim to be "life extinct". It was his expressed opinion at that time that the deceased had been killed some three hours previously.

'I asked another resident of the building to attend at Leman Street Police Office and inform the duty sergeant of what had occurred. I was relieved at my post by fellow constables and began enquiries at the White Hart public house, a few yards from the entrance to George Yard. The proprietor, a Mr Brougham, advised me that a lady answering the description of the clothing I gave him as being worn by the deceased was known to him as Martha Turner and lived at an address in George Street, Spitalfields. I made subsequent enquiries and located a Miss Jacobs, who advised me of the deceased's movements until approximately eleven o'clock on the previous evening. I was then involved in an attempt to identify a guardsman who is believed to have been in the company of the deceased at a time closer to her death, but without success.'

'Yes, thank you, constable,' Coroner Collier interrupted him, 'we'll get to that part of your evidence in just a moment. For the present, please describe the place where you found the body.'

'It's a doss house, sir. Sorry, I mean a common lodging house, of the standard layout. There's a staircase with landings, from which the individual rooms are accessed and the body was lying on its back on the first floor landing.'

'Was there anything to indicate that the deceased had recently been in any particular room?'

'No, sir. She was lying smack in the middle of the landing.'

'And you mentioned blood?'

'Yes, sir. Quite a lot of it actually, sir.'

'Did you gain the impression that the body had been moved since the wounds were inflicted on it? Anything to indicate, for example, that it might have been dragged onto the landing from one of the rooms?'

'No, sir.'

'Very well, now what can you tell this inquest about a guardsman?'

'Well, sir, when I spoke to the proprietor of the White Hart, he advised me that he'd seen a woman he believed to have been the deceased, along with another woman, heading off down the High Street, each of them in company with a guardsman. He knew the other woman very well, it seems, and was able to advise me that the deceased — or who we believe to have been the deceased, anyway — went off into George Yard with her man, while the woman he knew better carried on down the High Street with hers.'

'Who was this woman that the proprietor knew better than the deceased?'

'He named her as Pearly Poll, sir. That's the name she's known by, anyway.'

'And will this Pearly Poll be giving evidence to this inquest?'

'I've no idea, sir. Inspector Reid's in charge of the witnesses.'

'Very well. So I gather from your earlier testimony that you set out to find this guardsman. That was a bit like looking for a needle in a haystack, wasn't it?'

'Yes and no, sir. It just so happened that earlier that night — at around two am, it must have been — I had occasion to question a guardsman about his behaviour. He was loitering around the entrance to George Yard and when I challenged him he said that he was waiting for a friend of his. His precise words were: "No problems, sonny. I'm just waiting on a chum who went off with a girl down that way," and he pointed further on down the High Street. It wasn't until I spoke to the proprietor of the White Hart that it occurred to me that this must be the man who paired off with the deceased and so I went along to the Tower Barracks to see if I could see him again.'

'And were you successful?'

'No, sir.'

'Very well, you may stand down.'

The Coroner consulted his notes, then looked down encouragingly at Esther.

'Miss Jacobs, I believe you're next.'

Esther climbed into the witness chair, took a deep breath, recited the oath after the official had handed her the Bible, then smiled wanly back at the Coroner, who again consulted his notes.

'You are Miss Esther Jacobs, of Number 19, George Street, Spitalfields?'

'Yes, sir,' Esther replied, as her throat suddenly went dry.

'You'll have to speak up a little more loudly than that, Miss Jacobs,' the Coroner advised her. 'This is a fairly large room and it contains quite a lot of people who have nothing better to do with their time. If the jury are to hear you — and they're the ones on the benches beside me — you have to speak up a little more loudly.'

'Sorry, sir — I'm very nervous.'

'Yes, of course you are, but you have nothing to fear from speaking the truth. Unless, of course, you've been up to something you shouldn't.'

'I can assure you I haven't, sir.'

'That was my attempt at humour, Miss Jacobs. Now, you list your occupation as seamstress — is that correct?'

'Yes, sir.'

'And how did you come to know the deceased?'

'She was my neighbour, sir. She had the room across from mine in the lodging house.'

'These common lodging houses are notorious for their fluctuating populations. How long had you known the deceased?'

'Three or four months, sir, but we became very friendly during that time.'

'You'll forgive me for mentioning this, Miss Jacobs, but you seem to be a sensitive young lady of some education and breeding and yet the deceased appears to have been what we call an "unfortunate" in this polite society of ours. How well did you actually know her?'

'We spoke every day, sir, and we exchanged information about our previous lives. I know that she was what you called an "unfortunate" at one time, but she'd changed her ways since she met Harry — that's her husband — and I can't believe that she'd go off down a dark alleyway with a man she'd only just met.'

'As I understand these things, Miss Jacobs, it's not customary for prostitutes to ask their marks for references or formal introductions.'

There was general laughter and Esther blushed.

'I'm just saying, sir, that I believe that Martha was making every effort to live a decent life and on the night she was killed her husband was waiting for her at home.'

'I'm sure many a cuckolded husband has found himself in that unfortunate situation, Miss Jacobs, but be that as it may, did you have any reason to believe that the deceased was about to revert to her previous calling when you parted company with her?'

'No, sir. Quite the opposite.'

'Where was this?'

'In the snug bar of the White Hart.'

'Was she alone?'

'There was a group of other women at another table and half a dozen or so soldiers.'

'Guardsmen?'

'I wouldn't know, sir, except they were wearing army uniforms.'

'And what time did you leave her?'

'Around eleven o'clock, sir. She was meant to be following closely behind me.'

'But she didn't?'

'No, sir.'

'You felt no apprehension, leaving her there alone?'

'No sir. It was Bank Holiday and the place was quite crowded.'

'What reason, if any, did the deceased give you for not returning home with you, bearing in mind that it's well known that the streets of Whitechapel, and for that matter Spitalfields, are quite hazardous after dark?'

'She had business to discuss with another woman who was there as well.'

'Was this woman by any chance called "Pearly Poll"?'

'Yes, sir.'

'And you didn't see your friend again?'

'No, sir.'

'By what name did you know the deceased?'

'Martha Turner, sir. Wife of Henry Turner.'

'You've never heard her called Martha Tabram?'

'No, sir, although I believe she was married once before.'

'One final question. Did the deceased appear to possess any money that evening?'

'Enough to buy drinks, sir, although she did mention two small debts that she'd recently incurred.'

'Was she drunk when you left her?'

'I'm no judge, sir, but I couldn't say she was entirely sober.'

'Very well, thank you, Miss Jacobs. You may also stand down.'

As Esther took a vacant seat on the front row, she looked back up to see the coroner in a whispered conversation with Inspector Reid. The coroner looked up when he became aware that all eyes were upon them and he announced a ten minute adjournment.

Esther decided that she needed some air after her ordeal in the witness box and wandered outside, where she stood under the shade of an awning that projected from the window of a pie shop, deciding whether she might spare some coins for a mutton pie as she smelt the tempting aroma wafting out from the shop. Tradesmen's wagons rolled up and down the dusty cobbles of the busy thoroughfare, their iron wheels grinding out a cacophony of noise that all but drowned out the calls of the street hawkers. It was so noisy that she didn't hear the first tentative words from the police constable who sought to address her. It was only when he caught the elbow of her jacket that she realised that there was someone there and she started in alarm, then turned to look up into the bluest pair of eyes she could ever recall, set in an open, boyish face that was smiling at her beneath a police helmet.

'Sorry, miss, I didn't mean to startle you.'

'That's all right — you gave me a surprise, that's all.'

'I'm Constable Enright and I'm attending the inquest with Inspector Reid. I was interested to hear your evidence in there — you don't believe that your friend went off with a guardsman, do you?'

Esther shook her head. 'No, and what's more, I can't for the life of me make sense of what your colleague in there said about her being killed at two o'clock in the morning. I left her at eleven and according to the landlord of the White Hart, she went off with the guardsman not long after that. If she had been persuaded back to her old ways, which I doubt, it wouldn't have taken three hours, would it?'

'What wouldn't?' the constable asked cheekily and Esther blushed.

'What she was supposedly doing with the guardsman. And that's another thing — I know Martha could be pretty irresponsible when it came to drink, but she knew her husband was waiting at home and they'd been separated for a while, so she'd be glad to see him back and anxious to get home. The last thing she said to me was that she'd no intention of going back to totting and she was very nervous about that woman Pearly Poll.'

'I agree with you that the times don't add up and that's what Inspector Reid's thinking. But where do you think she was for those three hours?'

'Maybe Pearly Poll will be able to tell us.'

'She might, if we could find her,' he replied.

Esther's face set in a puzzled frown. 'But she's in the back row, along with one of the other women who were with her that night. I thought it a little odd that she wasn't sitting in the same row as me, waiting to give evidence.'

'You mean she's inside there, attending the inquest?'

'Yes, towards the back. Wearing a big black hat covered in feathers, next to a scrawny woman in a red bonnet.'

'Excuse me just a moment!' Constable Enright said excitedly as he scuttled back into the Institute.

Esther waited a few more minutes before going back in and when she did so she found herself moving against a tide of observers on their way out. Back in the room in which she had given her evidence Inspector Reid was talking to Pearly Poll, his hand on her arm in a restraining gesture and a stern look on his face. Constable Enright noticed Esther standing hesitantly in the doorway, smiled, and came back down the gangway between the chairs in order to speak to her.

'You were right! That's Pearly Poll and her friend and Inspector Reid is mightily indebted to the pair of us. The inquest's been adjourned until we can properly identify your friend.'

'She was Martha Turner — I told the Coroner that.'

'There's some suggestion that she may still have been married to her former husband. But you'll have to come back on another day if you want to be there for the rest of the evidence.'

'What day?'

'We don't know yet, since it'll depend on how much more evidence we can get. If you give me your address again, I'll be sure to let you know.'

Esther duly obliged, then walked back out, deeply troubled in her mind. She was no police constable, but none of what she'd heard seemed to fit the facts that she knew. And she still couldn't believe that Martha had gone back to her former life, when her future lay with Harry, who'd just come back to her.

She found herself approaching the front door of the White Hart and shuddered as she looked up into George Yard, where poor Martha had met her death. A brewer's cart was unloading barrels onto the narrow pavement and landlord Jack Brougham was helping the driver's boy roll them into his premises. He looked up as he saw Esther standing there and smiled. Encouraged, Esther followed him inside and waited until he came back up through the flap that led down to the cellar. He frowned as he saw her standing politely at the counter.

'We're not open 'till noon,' he advised her gruffly.

'I'm not here for a drink,' Esther advised him.

'That'll make a change,' Jack grinned. 'But if you're another one o' them from the orphanage, after money, I gave pretty generously last week, so sling yer 'ook.'

'Actually, I'm here for some information,' Esther was surprised to hear herself say.

'An' what sorta information would that be?'

'It's about my friend Martha — the one who was killed next door in that alleyway.'

'George Yard, yer mean? A queer sorta place is George Yard. All sorts of riff-raff collect in there.'

'You told the police that you saw my friend go into the Yard with a guardsman?'

'Yeah, so what?'

'Were there only the two of them, can you remember?'

'As best as I can recall, there was a whole crowd o' them left at the same time.'

'With Pearly Poll?'

'Yeah, that's right. She were in the lead, wi' a soldier of 'er own. I remember 'er tellin' the other woman — yer friend, it musta bin — ter take 'er mark inter George's Yard an' she'd go down the road a bit wi' 'er admirer. 'E were another guardsman.'

'The woman who went into George Yard — you told the police it was my friend?'

'I told the police what I'm tellin' yer now — it were a woman in a green dress. They all looks the bloody same ter me, ter be honest wi' yer.'

Esther's eyes opened wide. 'You said a green dress. Not a green skirt?'

'It's the same thing, int it?'

'No. My friend was wearing a green skirt and a black jacket. Are you telling me that the woman you saw going into George's Yard was wearing a green dress? You know, green all over, top and bottom?'

'Yeah, that's right, like I told the police.'

'The woman who went into George Yard wasn't my friend!'

'Then 'ow come she finished up dead in there?' George challenged her, as her face fell.

'I don't know,' Esther replied, 'but at least now I know that she hadn't gone back to her old life. Thank you very much, Mr ...?'

'Brougham. George Brougham.'

'Thank you, Mr Brougham. You may be getting another visit from the police.'

'I gets that every night, thank yer anyway,' Brougham grinned back as he took another incoming barrel from the brewer's boy and bounced it down the cellar stairs.

Chapter Three

Life returned to normal for Esther after all the excitement of the inquest. Day after day in her room, mending, shortening, lengthening, taking in and letting out garments with such mind-numbing regularity that she was beginning to think that everyone in East London was changing shape weekly. There was little to relieve the boredom and little to distinguish one day from another as she worked away in her chair by the window, making the most of the available daylight and occasionally glancing down at the spasmodic action in the yard below, where overripe sides of meat from local butchers were converted into cat-food. It was still summer, but unseasonably wet, so at least she wasn't obliged to open her casement window for coolness, letting in the nauseating smell from the yard below.

Harry Turner called in twice, in order to collect a few of his things from the room across the landing that he'd shared with Martha, but Esther gave him a wide berth, in case he somehow blamed her for the fact that his late wife had been drinking in the White Hart before she met her cruel end. Most of the time, as she sat working her deft fingers with needle, thread and scissors, Esther's mind would drift back to that fatal night and the facts that didn't add up. She told herself that she should advise the police of the mistaken identification of Martha as the one who'd gone off with the guardsman, but she wasn't entirely convinced in her mind whether this was to assist the police investigation into Martha's death, or simply to rescue her friend's reputation. Then one day she got her opportunity.

She got up when she heard the tapping on her door and when she opened it Sadie Thompson stood there with one of her disapproving looks.

'There's a bobby downstairs in the kitchen askin' fer yer. What yer bin up to, then? This is a respectable 'ouse, this is.'

'And I'm a respectable boarder,' Esther reminded her with a smile. 'It's probably more about Martha. Is the constable a good-looking young one with the most entrancing blue eyes?'

'I thought yer said yer was respectable?' Sadie countered. 'Best go down an' find out what 'e wants, afore yer give the place a bad name.'

Constable Enright had removed his helmet and was standing uncertainly by the sink, as Esther breezed in with her bag of tea and two cups.

'Would you like a cup of tea, constable?'

'Jack. Please call me Jack.'

'Very well, would you care for a cup of tea, Constable Jack?'

He grinned and she gestured for him to take a seat at the grimy table in the centre of the modest kitchen. He placed his helmet to the side as he sat down and Esther filled the pot and lit the gas before taking a seat across from him on the only other available chair.

'So what did you want to see me about?' she enquired.

'I'm here to tell you that the inquest resumes next Thursday — the twenty-third.'

'Will Pearly Poll be there?'

'She will if she knows what's good for her.' Jack grinned. 'Inspector Reid fair got stuck into her for not coming forward when we asked for information from the public. Seems that she hid herself away up west somewhere, then she was stupid enough to show her face at the inquest. And to top that, she made a complete mess of identifying the guardsmen they were with that night.'

'I meant to tell you,' Esther interrupted him, 'I spoke to the landlord of the White Hart and he as good as admitted that he identified the wrong person who went into George Yard with the other guardsman. It wasn't Martha at all.'

'Then how did she end up dead in there?' Jack enquired.

'I don't know. Do you take sugar in your tea? I've no milk, I'm afraid.'

'Just black with two sugars will be fine,' Jack assured her.

'What did you mean about Pearly Poll making a mess of the identification?'

'Well, we took her up to the Tower, her having missed the first appointment we made with her, mind you. We paraded dozens of guardsmen in front of her, then she suddenly seemed to remember that the guardsmen that night had white cap-bands.'

'So they did,' Esther recalled as her memory replayed the vision of the soldiers sitting at the table in the snug bar of the White Hart.

'Well,' Jack continued, 'that means that they were Coldstream Guards from the Wellington Barracks, not Grenadier Guards from the Tower. So two days later we did the whole thing all over again, this time at the Wellington Barracks and after a lot of stuffing around Poll picked out two blokes who turned out to have provable alibis. That took us back to where we'd started and for myself I'd say that Poll seemed pretty pleased about the outcome, almost as if she didn't want us to find the man responsible.'

'Does it not perhaps occur to you that Poll knows more about Martha's death than she's admitting?'

'That certainly occurs to Inspector Reid and we've detailed men to keep a closer eye on her. Trouble is that she always seems to be moving about from one lodging house to another. The current one's up this way, in Dorset Street, but the woman who runs the place is as tricky as a bagful of ferrets.'

'What do you know about Poll?' Esther persevered as she poured Jack a cup of tea.

'Inspector Reid's been looking into her and it seems that at one time she was a regular midwife. A proper one, that is, not one of those old crones that help out a neighbour during childbirth in some rat-infested hovel. She was highly regarded in Bethnal Green for some years, then it seems that she took to drinking and was warned off doing any more deliveries after a mother and her child died during a confinement while Poll was lying insensible on the floor.'

'Horrible!' Esther exclaimed as her face screwed up in revulsion.

'It gets worse, I'm afraid,' Jack warned her. 'Seems that now she operates a nice side-line in getting rid of babies.'

'What, murdering them you mean?'

'In a sense, but before they're even born. It's what the law calls abortion and in her other profession she probably gets a lot of calls on her talents with a knitting needle.'

'Ugh!' Esther reacted as she put down her tea cup and shuddered. 'Sorry,' she added sheepishly, 'you must think I'm a bit of a mimsy.'

'Not at all,' Jack assured her. 'After the gin-sodden old hags I normally have to deal with, you're a very refreshing change, believe me.'

'So, as well as running street prostitutes, Poll does abortions in her spare time?' Esther enquired with distaste.

'So it seems and Inspector Reid would give half his pension to catch her at it. Which reminds me, he has some questions for you.'

'Such as?'

'Are you sure that the woman who was sitting with Poll at the inquest was definitely with her on the night that your friend was murdered?'

'Definitely. She has a very distinctive scar on her head and she was wearing the same red bonnet. Why?'

'She's denying it and Poll seemed pretty keen to back her up on that.'

'Well, it was definitely her.'

'Good, next question — was your friend wearing the same clothes when she was killed as she'd been wearing when you last saw her?'

'Well, obviously I didn't see her body, thank God, but the other constable who gave evidence at the inquest said that she was wearing a green skirt and a black jacket and that's what she had on when I last saw her. Yet the landlord of the White Hart told me that the woman he'd seen going into George Yard was wearing a green gown. That's to say, the same colour top and bottom and all of a piece.'

'Excellent!' Jack enthused as he finished off the last of his tea. 'Inspector Reid noticed the discrepancy and gave Constable Barrett a right dressing-down for not knowing the difference.'

'It takes a seamstress like me to know the difference,' Esther smiled, 'and I don't suppose that the police want to send their constables to needlework classes.'

'No, probably not,' Jack grinned back. 'Anyway, thank you for the tea and now I'd better be getting back. You've answered my questions. Except …'

'Except what?' Esther asked.

'I was wondering if I could take you out on Sunday.'

'Oh!' Esther blushed.

'I didn't mean to cause you any embarrassment,' Jack said, apologetically.

'You just took me by surprise,' Esther replied, smiling shyly. 'I don't have any prior engagements so yes, that would be nice.'

Chapter Four

'My brother Abraham and I used to play hide and seek among the gravestones here,' Esther reminisced as they strolled slowly side by side through the churchyard of Christchurch the following Sunday afternoon. 'That was in the days when it was safe to walk the streets of Spitalfields, of course.'

'Older brother or younger?' Jack enquired.

'Older by two years. Last heard of in the army, somewhere in the Sudan. He hardly ever writes, although we both had a good education.'

'Forgive me for being inquisitive,' Jack ventured to ask, 'but with a good education, what led to your being a seamstress?'

'You're quite right to be puzzled,' Esther conceded. 'I had intended to be an artist or something else creative, but both my parents were drowned when the *Thames Lady* capsized six years ago. You may remember that incident, if you were in the police in those days.'

Jack chuckled. 'I must look older than I thought. In 1882 I was only fifteen.'

Esther did a quick calculation. 'So you're only twenty-one now? I'm two years older than you!'

'Does that matter?'

'For what?'

'For us walking out together like this?'

'Perhaps only if it develops into something deeper.'

'Do you think it might?'

'Tell me about your family,' Esther asked evasively.

Jack kicked out at a grass clump ahead of him as he replied. 'I'm half an orphan myself. My father died when I was 14, so about the same time that you lost both your parents. He was something in insurance in the City, so he left us fairly well provided for and my mother still lives in the house I grew up in, within sight of the Thames, in Barking. I have a sister, Lucy, who still lives at home, although she's seventeen now.'

'I'll ask you the same question you asked me,' Esther smiled. 'If you're from a well-heeled background, how did you come to be a humble police constable?'

'It's the first time I've ever been called humble,' Jack chuckled, 'but you can thank my Uncle Percy for the fact that I'm a bobby by profession. He's my father's brother and he took me to live with him and his family in Moorgate. He was a police sergeant at that time, stationed at Hackney, then he volunteered for the Detective Branch at Scotland Yard and was accepted. I was coming on nineteen then and fascinated by anything and everything to do with policing, so I signed up and found myself in Whitechapel. I've been there for two years come October and I have lodgings in Mansell Street, not far from where I work.'

'It's very rough down there, isn't it?'

'It can be, but I reckon that Spitalfields can rival it. Spitalfields is only considered more genteel because the Jews once owned most of it, although that's rapidly changing.'

'It certainly is,' Esther agreed. 'The people who took me in when my parents left me an orphan had their garment factory burned from under them, with me inside it I might add, when there was one of those periodic "Hate the Jews" campaigns. I had to move lodgings again and now there I am in George Street, taking in sewing and other alterations from the people I used to live with.'

It fell silent for a moment, but Jack felt that he had to ask. 'You mentioned a brother named Abraham and you're Esther

Jacobs. I wouldn't need the instincts of a trained police officer to work out that you're Jewish yourself, aren't you?'

'Yes — does that matter, as you asked me earlier?'

'And you replied "for what?" as I recall,' Jack reminded her.

Esther smiled as she replied, 'And your answer to that was "for us walking out together like this". It doesn't matter to me that you're two years younger than me, if it doesn't matter to you that I'm Jewish.'

Jack reached out for her hand and squeezed it, omitting to let go afterwards. 'I'm glad we've got that settled. I happened to notice, as we came in from Commercial Street, that there was a kiosk with a lemonade vendor. Let's go back there, get something to refresh ourselves with and sit on that bench near the entrance.'

Chapter Five

Esther spent the next few days in a dreamy haze, remembering every minute of her precious two hours in Jack's company, recalling every word of their conversation and counting the hours until the agreed repetition the following Sunday. Unfortunately, before that happy day dawned she felt obliged to attend the renewed inquest into Martha's death and she experienced a pang of guilt when she caught herself hoping that the solemnity of it would somehow not cast a shadow over the glow that seemed to hang around she and Jack when they were together and the natural affinity that had seemed to exist between them.

Thursday came around soon enough, but this time Esther was seated among the main body of those attending as the coroner formally announced the reopening of the adjourned proceedings. Things appeared to be different this time, however. The jury were still sitting on benches to the side of the coroner, but on his other side sat Inspector Reid and it was clear from the muted conversation between them that the inspector was intent on having his input into what was about to transpire. Esther looked around the room eagerly for a glimpse of Jack, who had not been anywhere in evidence when she first entered the room. She caught sight of him at the back, standing in a determined pose near the door through which people entered and left. She caught his eye and smiled and he smiled back and winked. Esther's heart began to flutter, seemingly of its own accord and her face flushed as she turned back to face the front when the coroner called his first witness.

A serious looking man in a dark frock coat and stovepipe hat took the oath and the coroner seemed anxious to show his respect as he smiled graciously at the witness, who had given his name as Dr Timothy Killeen.

'Doctor,' the coroner said obsequiously, 'we obviously had your preliminary report available to us on the first day of this inquest, but it is my understanding that you have now had the opportunity to finalise your report in connection with the post-mortem that you conducted on the body of the deceased on the morning of the seventh of August last. Are you able to give us your full opinion on cause of death at this time?'

'Indeed I am. I can confirm that what actually killed her was a deep wound to the chest, which was of such severity that it penetrated the sternum — that is, the breastbone — and ruptured the heart. But, in all, I counted some thirty-nine wounds to the upper and lower torso. Do you wish me to list them?'

'If you would be so good, doctor.'

'The left lung had been penetrated in five places and the right lung in two. There were five knife blows to the liver and two to the spleen. There were a further six wounds to the general area of the lower stomach. Any one of these wounds could, in due course, have proved fatal if left untreated, but it is my firm belief that the blow to the heart would have been instantly fatal. It may well have been inflicted first and in my opinion it was delivered by a dagger or bayonet, whereas the subsequent injuries might have been achieved with a mere penknife.'

'It is your opinion that there were two weapons employed?' the coroner queried.

'It is,' Dr Killeen replied. 'In my opinion, the perpetrator was a strong male and possibly someone with access to a bayonet or similar.'

'Such as a soldier?' the coroner enquired.

'Such a man would certainly be a likely suspect,' the doctor conceded.

'And I believe that your original estimate for the time of death was some three hours before your examination? Did you have subsequent cause to amend that opinion?'

'No. In my opinion she died at some time around two-thirty on the morning of the seventh.'

'One final question, if I may, doctor. When you examined the body of the deceased, did you find any evidence that she might recently have had a connection with a man?'

'No, sir.'

'Thank you, doctor. You may step down. The community is obliged to you for your work and for your attendance here today.'

Esther had listened with mounting horror to the description of the savagery of the attack on her friend and tried to imagine what Martha's final moments must have been like as she reached into the sleeve of her jacket for a handkerchief to stem the flow of tears. To distract herself temporarily, she gazed across at the side benches containing the other witnesses who had been called to testify on this second day and found herself staring at Pearly Poll. Her face was a mask of indifference as she glared up at the coroner, seemingly unmoved by what they had all heard. She betrayed no emotion whatsoever and Esther wanted to rush across the room and slap the cold-blooded woman.

'You are Henry Samuel Tabram, a foreman packer, of 6 River Terrace, East Greenwich?' the coroner enquired of the smartly dressed, grey-haired man who was the next witness.

'I am, sir.'

'And on the fourteenth day of this month, at the mortuary attached to Whitechapel Workhouse Infirmary, you identified the deceased as one Martha Tabram?'

'Yes, sir, I did.'

'What was your relationship with the deceased?'

'She was my wife, sir.'

'You were still married to her?'

'Yes, sir, but living apart these past thirteen years, on account of her drinking.'

'When did you last see her?'

'That would have been some eighteen months or so ago sir, here in Whitechapel Road. She tried to get money off me with some hard-luck story about being near starvation, but I knew that she had taken up with another man and that any money I gave her would be spent on drink as usual, so I bid her good-day and walked away.'

'Did you ever know your wife to engage in prostitution?'

'Not during the time she was with me, no, sir.'

'Very well, thank you Mr Tabram, and my deepest sympathies for your loss.'

'It is no loss, sir,' Tabram muttered as he left the witness chair and glared at Harry Turner before striding down the room and through the door next to which Jack was still positioned.

Next up was Harry himself, who gave his occupation as carpenter, before explaining that he currently out of regular employment and that he and Martha had been keeping body and soul together by engaging in street hawking of trinkets, handkerchiefs and pomade sachets.

'Were you and the deceased cohabiting at the time of her death?' the coroner enquired.

'Yes and no, sir. That is ter say, we'd bin tergether on and off fer some nine years, but I'd leave 'er from time to time on account of 'er drinking 'abits. We was actually living apart on the night she died.'

'When did you last see her?'

'That woulda bin the Saturday afore she died, sir. I come across 'er in Leadenhall Street an' I give 'er one an' sixpence ter get stock for us ter trade. That musta bin the money she was spendin' on drink the night she died.'

'When you were living together, did you have any suspicion that she might be engaging in prostitution?'

'None whatsoever, sir, an' she knew better than that. But when she was inter the drink, she 'ad some queer friends.'

'Anyone in particular?'

'None that I can call ter mind, sir, except that there Pearly Poll what can be found in the White 'Art most nights.'

'And she had no regular companions when she was sober?'

'Just the lass what lived across the landin' in our lodgin's. Esther, 'er name were.'

'And you know of no-one who'd want to kill Mrs Tabram?'

'Only me, some nights when she'd bin on the bottle.'

This last remark caused a ripple of mirth around the room, but Esther didn't think it funny. Harry was dismissed from the witness chair and the coroner then called in a loud voice for Mary Ann Connolly. Esther was wondering who this might be when Pearly Poll rose and walked across the room to take her seat as a witness. As she lumbered past her line of sight, Esther was reminded of the lady's sheer height and overall bulk and wondered how on earth she managed to attract marks when she was surrounded by more attractive women, such as Esther had seen in her company on the night that Martha died. And, for that matter, Martha had been what could politely be described as 'plump', so what was it about these women that attracted men?

Esther was aware that Inspector Reid had leaned across and engaged in a whispered conversation with the coroner, who looked sideways at Poll, asked her to confirm her real name and then advised her that: 'Inspector Reid requires that I formally caution you that while you are not obliged to say anything that might incriminate you when answering my questions, anything you do say today might be used against you in subsequent criminal proceedings. Do you understand that?'

'Course,' Poll replied with a defiant look directly at Reid. 'I ain't done nuffin' I'm ashamed of, I can assure yer o' that.'

'Very well. Are you married or single, witness?'

'Single.'

'And your current address and occupation?'

'35 Dorset Street, Spitalfields, not currently employed.'

'Are you also known by the name of "Pearly Poll"?'

'Yeah.'

'You knew the deceased Martha Tabram?'

'Yeah, 'cept I knew 'er as Emma Turner.'

'By whatever name you knew her, you and she were in company together on the late evening of the sixth of August last?'

'That's right — in the White 'Art, it were.'

'And were there others in your company?'

'Some other ladies of my acquaintance, yeah.'

'And did you make the acquaintance of any men that evening?'

'Sure did — a bunch o' sojers.'

'Guardsmen?'

'So I bin told — sojers, anyroad.'

'And once again I remind you of the caution I administered at the start of your testimony when I ask you what, if anything, transpired between you, the deceased, and these soldiers?'

Poll grinned lasciviously. 'We went up an alley in the way o' business.'

'And what sort of business would that have been?'

'Tottin',' Poll replied with a defiant smirk.

'Prostitution?'

'Yeah.'

'How exactly did this come about?'

'Well, them sojers come over to our table an' asked if we was interested in a "short time", as it's called, an' if we knew of anywhere where we could go. They obviously wasn't local, else they'd've known that there's lots o' places aroun' Whitechapel where yer can duck inter some alley or other — even lyin' down, if the money's right.'

The coroner went slightly pale in the face and raised his hand. 'Yes, thank you, I think we get the general picture. So what arrangement, if any, did you come to with these guardsmen?'

'Well one o' them 'ad 'is eye on Emma — Martha, that is — an' another of 'em fancied me, so we sets off down the road — the 'Igh Street, that is — an' I pointed Martha an' 'er man up the alleyway next ter the White 'Art, since there's a doss house up there what never locks its doors, so yer can go on one o' the landin's an' do it lyin' down. Then I took my gentleman friend to another alleyway further down an' we 'ad a quick knee-trembler.'

More laughter rippled around the room and the coroner appeared to blush. 'I won't ask you what a knee-trembler is, Miss Connolly, but is it your evidence that you had carnal connection with this guardsman?'

'Yeah.'

'And what did you do next?'

'Went back ter the White 'Art an' spent me fourpence on a large gin.'

'Did you see Martha Tabram again that night?'

'No.'

'When you got back to the White Hart, were the other friends of yours still there?'

'No, they'd scarpered, so I figured they'd mebbe got off wi' the other sojers.'

'But when you first left the White Hart with your guardsman, the only ones to leave with you were the deceased and her guardsman?'

'Yeah, like I said.'

'Thank you, Miss Connolly. I don't think I have any further questions, unless Inspector Reid here has any other matters he wishes to have clarified?'

He looked enquiringly at Reid, who shook his head with a slow smile. The coroner turned to address the jury. He first reminded them of the duty they had been called to perform and summarised the evidence, such as it had been. He left them in little doubt of what verdict he expected from them and without needing to withdraw their foreman duly confirmed their finding that Martha Tabram had been murdered by 'a person or persons unknown.'

The coroner thanked the jury for performing their public duty with such efficiency and dedication, then turned back to make a few concluding remarks for the benefit of the gentlemen of the press who had been making notes of the proceedings.

'I can only observe,' he commented, 'that the terrible fate that overtook the deceased illustrates only too clearly the risks taken by those we denote as "unfortunates" when they ply their trade in the dark alleyways of this most violent area of London. We can only conjecture what drives these miserable wretches to hawk their bodies for the few pence necessary to ensure that they have a roof over their heads for one more night, but nevertheless it is incumbent upon me, as one of Her Majesty's Coronial Officers, to underline the dangers that they thereby court. This case involved one of the most dreadful murders that anyone could imagine and the man who perpetrated it must have been a perfect savage to have inflicted such a number of wounds on a defenceless woman in such a way. Thank you, ladies and gentlemen, that concludes this coronial inquest.'

Esther sat for a moment, contemplating what the coroner had just said and saying a silent prayer for Martha, wherever she was now, while the other spectators filed back out into the mid-morning sun. She turned round, looking for Jack, but he was nowhere to be seen, so she walked slowly and sadly out into the street. Poll was on the pavement next to the pie shop, with several other women around her, and she smiled across at Esther. Then suddenly Jack was by Esther's side, taking her by the elbow and steering her in the general direction of Aldgate.

'Inspector Reid wants to talk to you,' Jack advised her.

Esther looked back towards the building they had just left. 'Isn't he still inside there?'

'Not now. His police wagon was waiting for him at the rear of the building and I saw it heading back to Leman Street while I was keeping an eye on Pearly Poll and making a note of the descriptions of her friends. But before the inquest even started this morning, he asked me if I could locate you and take you down to the Detective Office. He doesn't know we're walking out together, so please don't tell him.'

'Why, are you ashamed of me or something?' Esther enquired, heart in mouth.

'Of course not. It's just that I'm on duty and — well, we're not supposed to fraternise with witnesses. Inspector Reid thinks that you're important to his enquiries.'

'I've already told the coroner what I know.'

'Sometimes,' Jack explained as he steered her carefully through the milling traffic at the busy three-way junction of Whitechapel Road, Commercial Road and Leman Street, 'witnesses don't know how important their evidence is when they can't see the overall direction that a police investigation's taking. I learned that from Uncle Percy.'

'So if I'm a witness, does that mean we can't meet up again on Sunday, like we planned?'

'That's different,' Jack explained. 'I'm off duty on Sundays. The office is just ahead, on our right.'

He led the way up the front steps of the gaunt, soot-stained, three-storied building into a hallway whose gloom contrasted markedly with the bright sunlight they had just left. Off to the right, behind a metal cage grille, a uniformed sergeant was processing a pair of protesting drunks, even though it was only just past the middle of the day. From elsewhere in the building could be heard shouts, the occasional scream, and the barking of orders, as Jack led the way up the broad staircase onto the first floor landing, then down a corridor at the end of which was a tall glass-fronted door whose embossed letters announced that behind it might be found the 'Criminal Investigation Department'. Jack pushed the door open and held it wide while Esther slipped past his arm to go in ahead of him, then waited until Jack led the way again.

As they passed the open door to an office halfway down this corridor they heard a low wolf whistle and Jack stopped for a moment, poked his head through the open door and called out, 'Forget it, Billy — she's with me.'

At the end of this corridor was another glass door that was partly open, revealing behind it the stocky figure of a bearded man who at first glance resembled one of Queen Victoria's sons, but who Esther recognised as Detective Inspector Reid. He looked up as Jack tapped on the glass of the half-open door and announced, 'Miss Jacobs, Inspector.'

Reid waved them both in and offered Esther a seat in front of his desk, before glaring at Jack. 'There was a cable awaiting my return. The Yard are insisting on sending their own man down on this one. Name of Enright — any relation?'

'If it's Percy Enright, he's my uncle,' Jack admitted.

Reid snorted. 'Well, it would seem that I can't be trusted to investigate the simple snuffing of a back-alley tottie, despite all my years in the Detective Branch. But I suspect it's political, since I hear that the Home Secretary and the Commissioner are concerned that some Army maniac may be on the loose with a bayonet. Anyway, sorry, Miss Jacobs,' he concluded as he apparently remembered that he had a civilian visitor.

'How can I be of assistance to you?' Esther enquired politely.

Reid glanced at Jack. 'Constable Enright here tells me that you believe that the landlord of the White Hart identified the wrong woman going into George Yard with a guardsman on the night that your friend was killed.'

'That's right,' Esther confirmed, 'and you were at the inquest this morning, when Pearly Poll lied about leaving the premises with only Martha and the two soldiers. According to Jack

Brougham, a whole crowd of them left at the same time and the woman who went into the Yard with the guardsman was wearing a green gown, not a black jacket and green skirt, which is what poor Martha was wearing.'

'We think we know who the woman in the green gown was,' Reid informed her. 'Her name's Polly Nichols and she's terrified of speaking out against Pearly Poll, even though we offered her a bodyguard. We need you to identify her as having been among those women with Pearly Poll in the snug bar of the White Hart that night. Constable Enright assures me that you'll be able to do that.'

'You remember, Esther?' Jack reminded her. 'You told me on the first day of the inquest that the woman sitting with Pearly Poll had also been at her table on the night you met her with Martha. That was Polly Nichols.'

'Don't prompt the witness, Enright. And she's "Miss Jacobs" to you.'

'Sorry sir.'

'Jack — sorry, Constable Enright — is correct, sir,' Esther confirmed. 'It was the same woman. But what do you think really happened, bearing in mind that the women went off with the guardsmen shortly before midnight, whereas poor old Martha didn't die until two in the morning?'

'That remains a mystery at present,' Reid admitted. 'But I'm impressed by your powers of analysis, Miss Jacobs. If it was indeed Polly Nichols who went with the guardsman and that was around, say, midnight, then we can eliminate the guardsman as the murderer. Unfortunately that idiot of a coroner couldn't see beyond the end of his spectacles and he seems to have been sold on the idea that it must have been a man with a bayonet, since that explains the deep wound to the heart. But I never encountered a murderer yet who took two weapons to do his dirty deed and a strong man could have inflicted all those wounds, if determined enough. And if the stab to the heart came first, then whoever it was would have been fully energised, which explains why the remaining wounds seemed slighter. Put in simple language, the murderer was running out of energy, but not, it would seem, enthusiasm. I'm hoping that Polly Nichols can supply some clues when we find her again.'

'You've lost her?' Esther enquired, aghast.

'Let's just say that she's lost herself,' Reid replied. 'She left here, refusing any bodyguard and giving an address in Thrawl Street, Spitalfields. But when my men called to collect her two days ago, her lodging house keeper said that she'd moved out. That could be a lie, of course, and I have men watching the place in case she returns. But if by any chance you see her on your travels, be sure and notify the nearest constable without delay.'

'Thrawl Street's just around the corner from where I live,' Esther advised him, 'and I'll be sure to keep a look out for her myself.'

'Excellent,' Reid replied. 'And since you've confirmed my suspicion that Pearly Poll's been lying to us, I think that's all I need detain you with today. Constable Enright will see you safely home.'

Chapter Six

Sunday eventually came and Jack was eagerly awaiting her in the kitchen in his best brown suit with a cutaway jacket, shiny brown boots and matching bowler. Esther felt slightly outclassed in her blue jacket and skirt combination, with black lace-up boots, but it was all that she possessed that Jack hadn't already seen her in and it would have to do. Hopefully Jack was more interested in her conversation that her fashion taste, since it was conversation that she craved, particularly with so much churning around inside her head. She wanted to get to know Jack better before embarking on a more regular relationship and she wanted to learn more of the events that had taken her only friend from her in such a brutal fashion.

Once they were back among the tombstones, she wasted no further time. 'Is there any news of Polly Nichols? I've been looking out for her, but with no success.'

'Afraid not,' Jack replied, 'but it is Sunday, I am off duty, and I'm not supposed to fraternise with witnesses, remember?'

'You're holding my hand, all the same,' Esther pointed out, refraining from adding that he'd been doing that since they'd passed the end of George Street.

'As long as we're not discussing the case, you're not a witness, so I can fraternise with you,' Jack replied.

'So, if you let go of my hand, we can talk about the investigation?'

'Is that what you'd prefer?'

'Yes and no. I'd like to talk about the investigation, but I still want to hold your hand.'

Jack thought for a moment, then to her sudden alarm let go of her hand.

'Why did you do that?' Esther enquired sharply.

'Take hold of my hand,' Jack instructed her. She did so and he leaned in close and pecked her on the cheek. 'Now you're fraternising with me, so that doesn't count. Ask away.'

'Why do you think Polly's hiding from Pearly Poll?'

'We don't know for certain that she is,' Jack reminded her. 'For all we know, Polly's hiding her from us because she knows what happened when Pearly Poll went off with one of the guardsmen. Perhaps it was that guardsman who killed your friend.'

'But either way, that must mean that Polly knows something about Martha's murder that Pearly Poll doesn't want the police to know, mustn't it? Looks like she doesn't want to get done for organising a prostitution ring. I know you police politely look the other way when it's just one woman at it, but that you come down hard on those who run brothels. '

'You're remarkably well informed for a seamstress,' Jack teased her. 'But that's what Inspector Reid's thinking along the lines of. If Pearly Poll knows what really happened that night, then the friends who were with her must obviously know something as well and maybe Polly Nichols is hiding from the guardsman who did it, since she may have been the one who went off with either him or his friend.'

'Has your uncle arrived yet?'

'He starts tomorrow and Inspector Reid's not very happy.'

'Is he blaming you for the fact that he's been replaced?'

'He hasn't been replaced. They'll be running the case together, that's all.'

'But isn't Scotland Yard more important than Leman Street?'

'Strictly speaking no, since they're both just Detective Branches. But Scotland Yard tends to get called in when the case is regarded as a serious one.'

'Aren't all murders serious?'

'Of course they are, but this one has aroused concerns regarding the security of the armoury at Wellington Barracks.'

'The bayonet, you mean?'

'Yes, except in Leman Street we don't think a bayonet was necessarily what was used. You can penetrate a breast bone with a strong blow of an ordinary knife, even a penknife.'

Esther shuddered. 'It's horrible! Let's talk about something else.'

'You were the one who introduced the topic,' Jack reminded her. 'So what shall we talk about?'

'Have you ever walked out with another girl?'

'No. My mother wanted me to "pay attentions", as she called them, to the vicar's daughter when I was home one Christmas, but she was quite dull and all she could talk about was her older sister's children.'

'Was she pretty?'

'Not particularly. Not like you, anyway.'

'And why did your mother want you to pay your attentions to her? Does she want you to marry young and give her lots of grandchildren?'

'No, I think she just wanted to keep me at home and away from Uncle Percy's influence, along with the lure of the wicked city. And I think we can leave the grandchildren to sister Lucy — she has the men queuing up for her.'

'Is your mother religious?'

'No, just motherly, I suppose you could call it. She just wants the best for me, that's all. A good wife, a secure home, lots of children, a comfortable income and a safe occupation.'

'So far you seem to have disappointed her very deeply,' Esther chuckled.

'She hasn't met you yet,' Jack commented enigmatically and it fell silent. Without anything being said they retraced their steps and invested in two more lemonades. As they sat side by side on the bench, Jack looked down uncomfortably at his boots before breaking the silence. 'Promise me you'll find the nearest constable if you do catch sight of Polly Nichols?' he implored her. 'Please don't do anything silly, like go up and talk to her. The guardsman might be following her.'

'Am I that important to you?' Esther enquired hopefully.

'Of course.' Jack looked back up at the sun disappearing behind a bank of cloud to the west. 'It looks as if it'll come on to rain in a short while. I should be getting you back to your lodgings before it does.'

'Only if you'll come into the kitchen with me and let me make you a cup of tea,' Esther replied. 'Our time together is too precious to me to want to give up a minute of it.'

The sun was well down towards the western horizon before Jack finally took his leave, after they had almost worn out the pack of cards that was part of Esther's few remaining possessions from her childhood. Each of them was reluctant to be the one to say goodbye, but eventually Jack stood uncertainly in the doorway of the side entrance in the alleyway, shuffling from one foot to the other, before he finally summoned up the courage to ask, 'May I kiss your cheek again?'

'No, you may not,' Esther replied, then grinned as his face fell. 'You may kiss me on the lips instead.'

The following Friday Esther was finishing a delicate stitching operation on a torn ballgown bodice when there was an insistent knock on her door and the sound of Sadie Thompson calling her name. Esther opened her door and Sadie began tutting, before getting to the point.

'Yer young man's in the kitchen, but 'e's wearin' 'is uniform this time. It's one thing ter be walkin out wi' 'im when 'e's proper dressed fer that sorta thing, but what will folks think if they see yer wi' 'im in the street, an' 'im in 'is bloomin' uniform? They'll think yerv'e bin up ter somethin' yer shouldn't. Best go down an' see what 'e wants.'

Esther ran down the stairs, enthusiastic but puzzled, and remembered to slow down before she was tempted to race into the kitchen and appear too eager. Jack stood there twisting his helmet nervously in his hands. He seemed relieved to see Esther, who sensed that this was not the appropriate occasion to kiss him on the cheek.

'It's not Sunday,' she observed nervously, 'or was the prospect of walking out with me again so overwhelming that it couldn't wait?'

'Thank God you're still in one piece!' Jack stuttered.

'And why wouldn't I be?' Esher enquired.

'It's Polly Nichols,' Jack replied. 'She's been done in just like your friend Martha!'

Chapter Seven

Esther turned pale, grabbed the side of the kitchen table and lowered herself into the vacant chair. Jack moved swiftly from where he had been standing at the side of the sink and put a comforting hand on her shoulder.

'Are you sure it's Polly Nichols?' Esther enquired in a shocked whisper.

'Inspector Reid's convinced, although it's not his case.'

'But surely …?' Esher began.

Jack interrupted her. 'She was found in Bucks Row — that's "J" Division, Bethnal Green.'

'Then how do you know anything about it?'

'Uncle Percy was called out early this morning. He'd been lodging in the section house attached to Leman Street, and with him being Scotland Yard and all …'

'And he notified Inspector Reid?'

'Yes, when we got back from viewing the body in the local mortuary. It happened sometime during the night, apparently, and I'd just come on shift when Uncle Percy appeared and told me what had happened. I didn't know it was Polly Nichols then, obviously, but when Uncle Percy gave me a general description of the woman who'd been murdered — particularly the mark on her forehead — I told him that it might be her. Then I went down to the mortuary with him and confirmed it. There's a mark on one of her clothes that we can be traced to the Workhouse, so we might be able to get confirmation from that. But keep that to yourself, because it's not public knowledge yet.'

'I hope you didn't come up here to collect me to identify the body as well,' Esther shuddered.

'No, I just came up to make sure that you're safe. I'm supposed to be making enquiries at the doss house round the corner which was her last known address.'

Esther reached up to where Jack's hand was resting on her shoulder, took his hand and squeezed it. 'That was very sweet of you, Jack.'

'You're very important to me,' he assured her as he squeezed back, 'and it looks as if Polly may have been done in to keep her quiet.'

'By the guardsman, you mean?'

'Who else? And Pearly Poll may have been threatened with the same thing if she didn't lead the guardsman to her. That's what Inspector Reid's saying anyway, but he and Uncle Percy seem to be in disagreement on that point.'

'What does your Uncle Percy think?'

'He doesn't know what to think at the moment, but — look, this is not very nice, but Polly had been stabbed a few times, just like your friend Martha, and Scotland Yard are clearly of the belief that some maniac was responsible for both deaths, since the nature of the deaths is so similar.'

'If Inspector Reid's right, then it was still the work of a maniac, except that the maniac in question is a guardsman associated with Pearly Poll,' Esther pointed out.

'Uncle Percy won't accept that a woman could have been involved in something like that,' Jack explained. 'He's a bit old-fashioned in that way — thinks that all women are soft, gentle and lacking in physical strength. "Men stab, women poison" is an expression of his that I've heard him use lots of times.'

'So, if Polly was done away with because of something she knows about Pearly Poll and the guardsman, what made you think that I might be in danger?' Esther enquired.

Jack hesitated for a moment, then grinned one of his grins. 'I didn't, really. It was just an excuse to come and see you while I was on duty.' Instinctively he reached forward and pulled her towards him in a firm hug, which she made no effort to resist.

'None o' that in my kitchen, if yer don't mind,' came Sadie Thompson's stern voice from the doorway and they sprang apart guiltily.

Esther, red in the face, felt that some explanation was required. 'Jack — Constable Enright — was just here to advise me that a woman was murdered in Bethnal Green during the night and they believe that it may be connected to the murder of poor old Martha.'

'Then yer constable friend would no doubt be better employed in searchin' fer 'er killer an' not moonin' around in my kitchen,' Sadie replied.

Jack replaced his helmet and made for the door.

'Don't forget next Sunday,' Esther reminded his retreating back.

'As if I could,' he replied as he turned and grinned yet again, before touching his helmet peak in a gesture of respect to the two women as he made his way out into the passageway.

The two men were arguing furiously, but Detective Sergeant Enright was determined to pull rank.

'It's not your case, Edmund — it's not even your Division. It's precisely for cases such as this, which cross police divisions, that Scotland Yard was created.'

'But I have the local knowledge,' Reid objected, 'and if I'm right, then this case and the Martha Tabram case are connected.'

'I saw the body, remember?' Enright reminded him. 'The throat was quite severely slashed and when we got her clothes off it was obvious that whoever was responsible had been slashing away at the chest and stomach. From what I've been told, your victim was simply stabbed through the heart. This was more frenzied, believe me — a good job I'd had breakfast before I went down there.'

'But the coincidence is too great to overlook. A vital witness to the murder of Martha Tabram goes missing, then finishes up dead. What are the random chances of some lunatic waylaying the very woman we've been searching for during the past two weeks?'

'It's a different sort of attack. Perhaps you'd like to go and inspect the body for yourself? The post-mortem must be completed by now.'

'Who's the doctor?'

'The Divisional man — Dr Llewellyn.'

Reid snorted. 'I wouldn't get that man to treat my horse. Get him in here as soon as he's finished.'

'Once again, let me remind you that it's not your case.'

'And let me remind you that Constable Enright may be your nephew, but he's under my command. Don't take him on any more errands with you.'

Three hours later, Dr Llewellyn was demanding to know why, as Divisional Surgeon for "J" Division, he was being asked to describe his findings to an Inspector in "H" Division.

The man from Scotland Yard had told him that it might be important, but Llewellyn normally reported to Inspector

Spratling, as he had done already that morning and he had patients to see.

'As I already reported to Inspector Spratling,' Llewellyn said plaintively as he shook his head at the proffered tea cup, 'the wounds were very extensive and seemingly the work of a deranged lunatic. I first viewed the corpse on the pavement at Bucks Row and in my professional opinion the poor wretch hadn't long since expired at that point, to judge by the warmth of the lower extremities — the legs, in amateur language. Curiously, although her throat had been slashed twice — once in each direction — there was little blood loss and no marks of any struggle. From this I deduce that the victim may well have been rendered unconscious first, thus resulting in less of a blood flow from the severed carotid. This hypothesis is supported by the discovery of what appears to be the residual mark of a bruise along the lower jaw. Be that as it may, the real mystery began when we got her clothes off.

'It was if she'd been attacked by a medical student while he was intoxicated. There was a jagged wound, very deep, cutting through the tissue wherever it travelled from left to right across the abdomen. It was as if someone had been seeking to cut open the lower intestines and womb. There were also several downstrokes to the side, as if the target had been the kidneys. Plus one in the general area of the vagina.'

He paused for breath and Enright smirked at Reid triumphantly. 'See? Nothing like your first job, where there was a simple stab to the heart.'

'Plus another thirty-eight stab wounds around the chest and torso,' Reid reminded him. 'Probably inflicted with a penknife.'

'Whoever did this was not relying on a penknife,' Llewellyn asserted. 'He would have needed an entire set of surgical knives to achieve what I observed in the mortuary. And at least thirty minutes, which raises the interesting question of how the offender was able to do that in full public view on a city pavement at a time of day when people were beginning to pass to and fro on their way to work. Dockers, meat handlers, draymen and so on. But there was no blood in the general location of the corpse to indicate that she had been carried there from elsewhere. I looked once they'd taken the body by handcart to the mortuary, on my instructions.'

'Could it have been done with an army bayonet?' Enright enquired.

Llewellyn shook his head. 'From what I've seen of those things, they're far too broad and blunt. One specially sharpened, possibly, but I doubt it. Those incisions are never, in my experience, seen outside medical school or hospital.'

'So perhaps a demented medical student?' Enright enquired.

'Dear God, I sincerely hope not,' Llewellyn shuddered. 'But someone with medical experience anyway. They were working in the half light and made no obvious cuts in her clothing. She was wearing several petticoats, a pair of drawers and some loosely fastened stays. Somehow or other, the person responsible managed to work under all of those, in the half light. Working by feel, that is, which requires a knowledge of human anatomy not normally possessed by your average slaughterman or Thames bargee. The absence of blood on her clothing also supports my theory that she was dead before this crude surgery commenced. Or at least, one would have to hope so.'

'Satisfied?' Enright gloated as Dr Llewellyn grumbled out of Reid's office, after demanding to know who to submit his account to.

Reid shook his head. 'Far from it. Remember that some army men are trained in battlefield first aid.'

'I have to make my report to Abberline,' Enright announced abruptly, 'so if you'll excuse me ...'

'Not Fred Abberline?' Reid demanded.

Enright nodded. 'It's an unusual name — how many other "Abberlines" do you think the Yard possesses?'

'He was the Inspector here when I first got out of uniform,' Reid advised Enright with a smile. 'At least he has local knowledge.'

'And so will I, by the time this is finished,' Enright reminded him.

'Well don't use any of my constables in order to get it. And when you next see your nephew, tell him to report directly to me. I have a job for him.'

Chapter Eight

It was raining heavily the following Sunday, so Jack was persuaded to remain in the kitchen, playing cards with Esther. For a short while, when the downpour briefly subsided, they went out for some air, during which time they were able to hold hands for the length of George Street and exchange a few furtive kisses in the doorway of the chandler's shop in Thrawl Street, until ordered to move on by the irate proprietor. Back in the kitchen, Jack looked thoughtfully across at Esther when it was her turn to shuffle the deck and enquired, 'Next Sunday, if it fines up, would you like to go walking down by the river?'

Esther grimaced. 'It's a bit sooty and grubby down there. Not to mention the smell and the noise.'

Jack grinned. 'I was thinking of further downriver, not down by the docks. There's a ferry from Tower Steps to Creekmouth, in Barking and we can walk up the bank. I know the area like the back of my hand and I used to go fishing in the creek. It's a healthy country walk.'

Esther looked doubtful. 'Sounds lovely, but you're forgetting that my parents were drowned on one of those things.'

'That was a pleasure boat, from what you tell me,' Jack countered. 'The ferries are much sturdier and better handled. They have to be, by regulation.'

'All the same ...' Esther wavered.

But Jack wasn't about to be put off. 'Give it some thought, anyway. You've got a whole week, although maybe you'll have decided by tomorrow. I haven't mentioned tomorrow yet.'

'I have some urgent orders to complete,' Esther advised him, 'and I think Mrs Thompson might get a bit huffy if you come round every day.'

'I'll be in uniform tomorrow,' Jack reminded her.

'That's even worse,' Esther objected and was met by another of Jack's entrancing grins.

'I'll also be on official business. Inspector Reid wants to see you again.'

'Is this you "fraternising" again?' Esther teased him.

'I'm serious. He wants you to look at some photographs.'

'Not the ones of that poor Polly's body, I hope?' Esther enquired with a shudder.

'No — prostitutes, from what I could make out.'

'Why?'

'He didn't say,' Jack advised her, then looked out of the window and smiled. 'It's stopped raining again. Fancy another stroll to the chandler's shop?'

'Thank you for taking the time, Miss Jacobs,' Inspector Reid said to Esther as he beckoned in the sergeant carrying the tea things. 'Tea?'

'Thank you, that would be very nice.'

'And perhaps a ginger biscuit?'

'That would be even nicer, thank you.'

'Constable Enright should be here in just a moment, along with his uncle, who's from Scotland Yard. He's been sent to teach me my job, it would seem, but we won't worry about that. It's just that I want you to look at some photographs and see if you recognise anyone.'

'Jack — sorry, Constable Enright — said that they were photographs of prostitutes.'

'That's correct. I just need to know if you can identify any of them as having been with Pearly Poll on the night that your friend Martha was murdered. Ah, here they come now.'

Jack came in accompanied by a tall, slim man who simply had to be his uncle, Esther concluded. The man had Jack's blue eyes and fresh complexion, although his once fair hair was now largely grey at the sides. He smiled knowingly down at Esther as Jack introduced them and Esther was wondering whether Jack had made any mention of their 'fraternising' when Inspector Reid interrupted her thoughts.

'The large book under Detective Sergeant Enright's arm is our library of mug-shots of local prostitutes. Whenever we run one in, we take the precaution of photographing them for future reference and a larger collection of raddled old hags you won't find anywhere else in the Metropolitan Police files. Take a look at this lot if you would, Miss Jacobs, and see if any of them are familiar to you from that evening before Martha Tabram was murdered.'

'That was several weeks ago now,' Esther reminded him in her own defence, 'but I'd be happy to try.'

There were some fifty pages or so of photographs of rough-looking women glaring angrily at the photographer, with accompanying images of their side profiles. Esther was unpleasantly astonished to learn how many there were plying the streets of Whitechapel — and these were only the ones who'd got caught, she reminded herself as she gloomily turned one page after another. Finally she turned the last page and sighed. 'I'm sorry — it was so long ago now. Was it really important?'

'Inspector Reid seems to think so,' Percy Enright replied dismissively.

'Inspector Reid *knows* so,' Reid replied defiantly. 'If we assume that Polly Nichols was murdered in order to silence her regarding something that happened on the night that Martha Tabram was murdered, then the next victim could turn out to be another of those women who were with her in the White Hart that night.'

'That's at least two assumptions,' Percy Enright observed. 'The first assumption is that there'll be another victim and the second — and bigger — assumption is that this elusive guardsman who's being guided around the district by Pearly Poll is capable of inflicting the sort of injuries that I witnessed on the body of the Nichols woman.'

'The Sergeant's of the opinion that we're looking for a maniac with more medical knowledge than is possessed by your average soldier,' Reid explained to Esther.

'Senior Scotland Yard officials share that opinion,' Enright insisted.

'Only because you gave it to them,' Reid growled back.

'I'm sure that Miss Jacobs has better things to do than listen to us argue over theories that shouldn't be expressed outside police hearing,' Enright said. 'Would you care to take one more look at those photographs, miss?'

Esther did as requested and halfway through the book there was one that caught her attention. More than anything she was struck by the woman's plainness of features and once again found herself wondering why men found such women so attractive that they would pay to engage in sexual activities with them, when most of them no doubt had loving wives at home. This one — whose name was given as 'Dark Annie' — had a noticeably thick nose and lips, and even allowing for the fact that she was presumably not pleased to be having her photograph taken she still seemed somewhat sullen of countenance.

'Was she one of them?' Reid enquired eagerly as he saw her staring at the photograph.

Esther shook her head. 'Definitely not. The others were all quite attractive, in a gaudy sort of way.'

'No-one looks their best in the early hours of the morning, after a hard night's totting,' Reid explained. 'Anyway, if you're certain that you haven't been able to pick anyone out, we'll call it a damp squib. Thank you anyway. Constable Enright will no doubt be happy to show you out.'

'I'm sorry,' Esther replied as she rose to her feet, feeling somehow inadequate. She was still feeling despondent as she walked back down the hallway from Reid's office and Jack looked sideways at her gloomy face as he attempted to lift her mood.

'Never mind. My uncle took quite a liking to you, I could tell.'

Esther was pondering his words as she walked slowly back up Whitechapel High Street, glancing through the open doors of the White Hart as she dodged a couple of street hawkers trying to interest her in boot laces. With a start she recognised the face of the woman seated at the bar and on a whim she walked on a few more paces, then stopped and sidled into the doorway of a cobbler's shop and waited.

Her patience was rewarded only a few minutes later when the woman walked unsteadily out of the White Hart and weaved her way into George Yard. Esther now had an urgent decision to make; should she follow the woman and find out why she'd gone into the Yard where Martha had died, or should she enter the White Hart and try to find out more about her? Then again, why should she do either of these things? Perhaps because she was becoming more fascinated by the week with this detective work and she had nothing better to do. And if she found out anything of value to the police, that would be a good enough excuse to see Jack again before next Sunday. She wanted to tell him that a walk along the creek in Barking was her greatest ambition at this point in her life, but she didn't want to seem too eager.

Somehow the prospect of wandering into that gloomy alleyway, with its horrible associations, didn't immediately appeal to her, so she took a deep breath, tried to look more confident than she felt, which wasn't difficult, and strode through the open door of the White Hart. There was no sign of the proprietor with whom she'd spoken on the previous occasion, whose name she couldn't remember anyway in her nervousness, but the younger man behind the counter seemed pleasant enough and the place was half empty anyway.

He smiled as Esther took a seat on one of the available seats at the long counter and ordered a small glass of mild beer.

'Heavy night last night, were it?' the barman enquired with a knowing grin.

Esther smiled back as she replied. 'I don't normally drink.'

'Then what brings you in 'ere at one o'clock in the afternoon, miss?'

'I need some information from you. That woman who was sitting in the seat I'm now occupying — did you know her?'

'What, Dark Annie, d'yer mean? There can't be anyone within a mile o' this place what doesn't know 'er. Are you one o' they Salvation Army types, tryin' ter save fallen women? If so, yer'd best follow Annie inter the alleyway next door, where she usually falls.'

'Does she live there?'

65

'Who knows? But she's often seen around there an' I 'eard tell that she 'as a room up in that doss 'ouse at the end.'

'Thank you very much,' Esther enthused as she smiled warmly at her informant. 'How much for the drink?'

'On the 'ouse,' the barman replied. 'I don't normally get ter talk ter a pretty face like yourn this early in the day. If yer really do save fallen women, save one fer me fer later.'

Esther could barely contain her excitement as she dashed back down the High Street and took her life in her hands by weaving in and out of the busy wagon traffic at the massive junction that gave access to Leman Street. Less than ten minutes later she was pressing up to the metal grille just inside the entrance to the Police Office and asking to speak to Constable Enright.

'He's out on patrol, miss. Would his uncle do instead? He's from Scotland Yard.'

'No, perhaps Inspector Reid, if he's not too busy.'

'I'll send up for him, miss, if you'd like to take a seat on that bench opposite.'

Esther was still trying to convince herself that she was not wasting anyone's time and trying to think of some way in which Dark Annie's association with George Yard might have a bearing on Martha's murder there weeks previously, when she was conscious of someone looking down at her. It was Jack's Uncle Percy and she smiled up at him.

'I thought you were on your way home,' he smiled back. 'Or were you waiting for Jack, by any chance? He's taken quite a shine to you, by the way. Don't go breaking his heart, else you'll answer to me.'

'I won't, I promise,' Esther assured him, as she willed her own heart to stop fluttering. Then a loud voice called her name and Inspector Reid came striding down the stairs. Percy

Enright looked up, frowned and bid Esther a good morning as he strode purposefully out through the front entrance.

'Did you change your mind about the identifications?' Reid enquired hopefully as he stared after the retreating Percy Enright, then smiled down at Esther.

'No, but ... look, this may mean nothing, but that woman whose photograph we were discussing earlier this morning — Dark Annie?'

'Yes, what about her?'

'I saw her coming out of the White Hart as I was walking back home. She went into George Yard and I made enquiries. I was told that she may have a room in the doss house in which they found Martha's body and it struck me as too much of a coincidence.'

Reid's eyes opened wide in respect. 'You have the instincts of a trained detective, Miss Jacobs. Come back upstairs with me. Just wait there a second while I give out some instructions.' He walked swiftly over to the grille cage and issued a loud command. 'Get Enright back off patrol and in here. The nephew, that is, not the spy from the Yard. Then get a four man squad together and make sure they've all got their truncheons.'

An hour and more tea and biscuits later, Esther looked up from the comfortable armchair in which she'd been installed in the tea room, to the obvious delight of several constables who came and went, when a tall shadow fell across the open doorway and there stood Jack.

'You've really lit a fire under the Inspector! We're off to flush Dark Annie out of her rat-run and bring her in for her own safety. You can't come with us, of course, but I was wondering if you'd had any other great inspirations while you've been sitting there.'

'Yes,' Esther replied. 'First of all, you have a lovely uncle. Secondly, I feel like a walk up a creek in Barking on Sunday afternoon.'

Chapter Nine

'We can take the train back, if this isn't to your liking,' Jack offered as he saw Esther's nose wrinkling in distaste.

'It's a bit smelly, you must admit,' she said.

'That's because the tide's out and the seaweed comes up on every tide,' Jack explained as he guided her by the elbow around a puddle that lay ahead of them on the bank of the creek as it wound its way up to distant Barking. 'It's getting all industrial now, but when we first moved here it was just like being in the country. The same railway that allowed my father to be in the City in less than an hour — which is why he chose to move here — also brought industry.'

'Can we "fraternise" now?' Esther enquired. 'I'm all agog to know what you found out when you took that party of constables into George Yard.'

'I didn't want anyone on the ferry to overhear us,' Jack advised her with an air of mystery and intrigue, 'because what we found out's supposed to be kept secret. I shouldn't even be telling you.'

'If it weren't for me, you'd never even have known that the Yard held a secret,' Esther pointed out, 'so the least you can do is to share it with me.'

'Well,' Jack explained, 'we went in there immediately after I left you at Leman Street and we found Dark Annie in no time, since she was lying unconscious on the stairs. Seems that she's been staying in a room there for the past week or two, but we ran her in for her own protection — or at least, that's what Inspector Reid told her.'

'The room she was staying in,' Esther butted in, 'was it by any chance on the first floor landing?'

'How did you guess?'

'You're not the only one who can put two and two together. Martha was killed on the landing between two room doors in there and Dark Annie's got a room somewhere in that dreadful place. All we need to do is find evidence of some sort of association between Dark Annie and Pearly Poll and her guardsman friend, and wouldn't it then be just too much coincidence if it was one of those rooms outside which Martha met her horrible fate?'

'Well deduced,' Jack replied as he used the occasion to take her hand back into his.

'Please don't hold my hand, if it means that's an end to our "fraternising",' Esther requested. 'You're just getting to the interesting bit. I was right, wasn't I?'

'Yes and no,' Jack replied, 'but as for "fraternising", I don't give a damn if we are, and you've given us enough help already, so I don't think you count as "the public" any more.'

'Delighted to hear it,' Esther sniffed, 'but get on with it, before I explode with anticipation!'

For the third time since they'd left the ferry, Jack looked up at the sky before replying. 'Dark Annie did indeed have a key to a room on that first floor landing, but she's not the only one, by all accounts. We finally tracked down the old bag who passes for the Superintendent of that particular rat-house and she told us that women are coming and going all the time in and out of that room. The rent's paid in advance, monthly, by "some Army gent", as she described him and provided that the rent's paid up to date neither she nor the proprietor seem to give a damn. I ran the Superintendent past Inspector Reid, who threatened her with a charge of "living off" and she just laughed in our faces. In the end we sent her packing with a formal warning.'

'Is that all you intend to do?' Esther demanded, 'The "army gent", as you call him, is almost certainly the guardsman you're all looking for and he's probably running the brothel in there, with Pearly Poll as his manageress. And why do you keep looking up at the sky? Are you apprehensive that we might be overheard by someone in one of those "dirigible" things?'

'I was just thinking that it looks like rain,' Jack replied evasively as they continued up the left hand bank of the creek as it slowly narrowed towards the distant houses.

'I'm not easily distracted, as you'll discover,' Esther persevered, 'so don't try and change the subject. What further enquiries do you intend to make in George Yard?'

Jack sighed. 'I really shouldn't be telling you this, but we already had some inside information that one of the rooms in George Yard is where Pearly Poll does her abortions. It's only rumour, mind, and it came from one of our criminal associates who's prepared to give us street-level information in exchange for not being charged with pick-pocketing from time to time. It's amazing what those street dips learn while they're hanging around waiting to snaffle a wallet.'

'So can't you just kick down all the doors and find out?' Esther enquired. 'And you were right — here come the first few spots of rain.'

'Follow me,' Jack replied with a smug look on his face as he pulled her by the hand, then ducked off the grassy stream bank through a hole in the wild privet hedge. He led the way up a muddy lane towards a fine three-storey house that sat in its own grounds next to the ruins of an old church, lifted the latch on the front gate and strode towards its front door.

Esther hesitated at the gate and Jack looked back and beckoned her into the front garden.

'How do you know we'll be allowed to shelter in there?' she demanded from the safety of the front gate.

'For one thing, it was once a vicarage and clergymen always give sanctuary to travellers in need,' Jack replied, 'and, more importantly, I grew up here.'

Esther walked up the path to join Jack as he knocked imperiously on the front door. It opened to reveal a young girl dressed in the standard black dress and white apron of a domestic servant, who smiled and stood back to let them in.

'Good day, Master Jackson,' she beamed, just as a tall, almost statuesque, woman in her early fifties, with striking white hair and piercing blue eyes, appeared in the hallway behind her, strode forward and all but lifted Jack bodily off the ground as she hugged him to her.

'Jackson, for once you kept your promise!' she enthused, as she looked past to him to where Esther stood transfixed. 'And you must be Esther — so glad you could finally make it! Do come inside and Alice will make us some tea, won't you Alice?'

Alice bowed slightly and disappeared further inside the house, while their hostess, who Esther took to be Jack's mother, escorted them into a finely appointed sitting room with several comfortable chairs and at least one sofa, all upholstered in the same heavy chintz rose pattern that exactly matched the curtains. As they took a seat, Esther silent mouthed 'Jackson?' to the man she knew as Jack, then remembered her manners as she caught his mother eyeing her up and down.

'This is very hospitable of you, Mrs Enright,' she mumbled.

'Constance, dear — do please call me Constance. "Mrs Enright" is so formal, and I hardly qualify for that name any more, since Jack's father has been dead these seven years or so. So, how was your journey down here?'

'It would have been better at high tide, I believe,' Esther replied in her best English.

Constance smiled. 'You are very tactful, Esther. The river stinks to high Heaven these days and the creek mouth is even worse, but for some reason Jackson seems to find it entrancing.'

'All those boyhood memories,' Jack explained, just as a vision of loveliness appeared in the doorway from the hall, with a petulant expression on an otherwise flawless countenance. She was so obviously Jack's sister, with her bright blue eyes and hair the colour of ripening corn.

'This is my sister Lucy,' Jack explained unnecessarily, 'but she normally has a smile for visitors.'

Lucy broke into a smile that reminded Esther of a torch beam. 'I'm sorry, please excuse me, but I've just made a very vexing discovery.'

'You mean the doctor's son's already spoken for?' Jack teased her, evoking a grin that must be an Enright family heirloom, Esther concluded.

'No, but almost as bad as that,' Lucy continued. 'I'm due to attend a social evening at the church after Evensong and Simon Molyneux will be there. I was hoping to wear that blue silk gown that I save for special occasions, but it's been so long since I had an opportunity to wear it in this backwater that when I tried it on earlier I discovered that I must have grown a couple of inches since last time. I can't possibly wear it, because then my ankles would be showing.'

'Does it have a hem?' Esther enquired without thinking.

'A what?' Lucy enquired.

'A hem — a fold of material running up the bottom of it, on the inside.'

'I believe so,' Lucy replied. 'Why do you ask?'

'Because it can be unpicked and let down, giving the gown extra length, depending on the width of the hem. I could let it down for you, if you'd permit me.'

'We don't have a sewing machine,' Constance Enright advised Esther with a smile.

'Neither do I, at home,' Esther replied, 'but I've done dozens by hand in the past.'

'That would be wonderful!' Lucy exclaimed and rushed out of the sitting room, returning a minute later with an exquisite blue silk tea dance gown. Esther asked for needle, thread and scissors and set about unpicking the two inch hem on the bottom.

'It'll need to be ironed when I've finished, but make sure that the iron's not too hot for this delicate silk,' she advised Lucy.

'You clearly have a talent for such matters,' Constance Enright complimented Esther as she poured the tea and helped herself to one of the buttered muffins that Alice had just placed on the side table. 'Are you in the garment trade?'

'I was, once,' Esther replied evasively, 'and I still am, in a manner of speaking.' She shook her head when Constance held the muffin plate towards her. 'I wouldn't want to get butter all over this beautiful gown,' she explained.

'Your parents have a clothing manufactory?' Constance enquired of Esther, but it was Jack who seized the initiative.

'Esther is an orphan, Mother.'

'They were cloth importers,' Esther added. 'But later, after they died, I was sort of adopted by the Rosens of Spitalfields, who taught me all about garment manufacture and repair.'

'And do you still reside with the Rosens?' Constance persevered.

'Mother!' Jack objected, but Esther was determined not to be spoken about as if she had no tongue of her own.

'The Rosens had their premises burned out by those who hate Jews.'

'And what is your opinion of Jews, Esther? That's a Jewish name, isn't it?'

'That's quite enough, Mother!' Jack insisted. 'Once Esther has finished her delicate work on Lucy's gown, we shall have to be leaving, so please bring me up to date on family news.'

'Very well, dear,' Constance agreed as she smiled reassuringly at Esther. 'Your cousin Emily is expecting again, but then my sister's daughter seems to enjoy being in almost constant childbirth. Twice was enough for me, obviously, but I have cause to be grateful for the pain and indignity of labour, since it gave me two such beautiful children. I hear that your Aunt Beatrice has an infection of the lungs that has laid her low again, but no doubt your Uncle Percy has kept you well advised of that. He informs me that he has been drafted in to work with you in connection with two horrible murders, the second barely a week ago. As you know, I disapprove heartily of your being involved in such sordid matters, but I have never been one to stand in the way of my children's desires, within reason. Fortunately, Lucy has shown no inclination to leave home as you did, although no doubt that will occur when she finally decides which of her would-be suitors to favour.'

'She's very beautiful,' Esther murmured, her head bowed low over her delicate stitching operation. 'There,' she announced with a triumphant smile, 'it's good enough for one evening's wear at least, but it should really be strengthened by a second row done with a sewing machine.'

'The least Lucy could have done in the circumstances,' Constance complained, 'was to remain in our company and watch how you did it, then give you her most heartfelt thanks. Instead, she's probably in her room, lost in one of those dreadful novel things that she's always reading. Do you read much, Esther?'

'We have to go now, Mother,' Jack announced with evident relief. 'We'll take the train back and it's stopped raining, so we can walk down Church Lane to the station. I take it that the trains still run on a Sunday?'

'I wouldn't know, dear,' his mother explained.

'They do, at least until six in the evening,' Lucy advised them as she reappeared in the doorway and caught the final part of the conversation. She took the gown from Esther and examined the new hem, then held it up to herself and looked down with a sigh of satisfaction. 'It looks perfect, thank you, Esther.'

'You planned that from the very start, didn't you?' Esther said accusingly as they walked down the lane towards the station.

'Mother insisted on meeting you,' Jack replied in his own defence.

'And why would that be?' Esther demanded. 'And why did your mother look me up and down as if she was hiring me as a domestic?'

'You can blame Uncle Percy for all of that,' Jack explained. 'He's taken quite a shine to you and he's obviously put two and two together and told Mother that at long last I've found a suitable young lady.'

'But I'm not "suitable", as you choose to call it, am I?' Esther objected. 'Your mother seemed to regard me with great suspicion and Lucy only took to me because I was able to alter her best party dress. The house is beautiful, even more than the house I grew up in before my parents were killed, and there's clearly a family of considerable breeding living in it. And here I am, a Jewish orphan living in a rooming house and taking in sewing to keep body and soul together.'

Jack stopped walking, turned to face Esther and leaned forward to kiss her on the lips. 'You're "suitable" as far as I'm concerned and I can read my mother. She's intrigued by you, obviously, and she rightly surmises that you're very important to me. As I once told you, she's only concerned for my happiness.'

'But ...'

'But nothing, Esther Jacobs,' Jack interrupted her as he placed two fingers on her lips to silence her. 'I've never met anyone who made me feel the way I do about you. I don't know whether it's ... well, it might be ...'

'Lost your tongue all of a sudden?' Esther teased him with a broad smile.

Jack turned bright red in the face and studied the ground on which they were standing. 'My mother's not the only one intrigued by you, Esther,' he mumbled, before looking back up, then directly down into her eyes. 'But for me, it's ...'

'It's what?' Esther encouraged him.

'It's something more. I've no experience of these things, but I think I may have fallen in love with you, Esther.'

Chapter Ten

'At least this one's on my patch,' Edmund Reid muttered as he looked down gloomily at the prostrate and mangled remains to the left of the steps leading down into the rear yard of 29 Hanbury Street. It was shortly after six thirty on that Sunday morning and Reid had been summoned from his bed by a breathless constable sent by police wagon from Commercial Street, where the discovery of the body had first been reported. Another constable called in from beat patrol in nearby Brick Lane had recognised Dark Annie as the lady he'd recently helped to take into protective custody at Leman Street.

'You're welcome to this one,' Inspector Chandler assured him with a grimace as he watched police surgeon George Phillips gingerly prodding and poking around the bloody corpse.

'Just don't tell Enright until I've had chance to alert the Yard direct,' Reid requested. He looked down as Phillips stood back up and straightened his back in the cold September morning air. 'Well?' he demanded.

Phillips shook his head. 'Difficult to tell, at this stage. Throat cut, obviously, but the torso's been messed around with as well. She's not stiffening yet, but not far off it. No obvious signs of a struggle and it probably happened in the past couple of hours. As I say, difficult to tell, but if the carotid was severed like that to begin with, she probably lost quite a lot of blood first off, some of which you can see on the ground near the neck and on that fence. Given that and the cool of the morning, the rigor would set in more quickly. That may also explain the relative lack of blood where the maniac set about carving like she was the Sunday roast.'

Reid moved off the bottom step and took a closer look. Annie was lying flat on her back, her head close to the rear wall of number 29 and her feet pointing towards the outbuildings at the bottom of the yard. Her skirt and petticoats were up around her waist and her knees were drawn up towards her middle with her feet on the ground, in a grotesque pose suggestive of intercourse.

'What's that on the shoulder of her jacket?' Chandler enquired.

'Her guts, in layman's terms,' Phillips replied.

Chandler went white in the face and began dry-retching.

Reid opted to get as much information as he could before Chandler began to void the contents of his stomach, as he was threatening to do. 'Any witnesses?'

'My men are rounding up the ones we know about and conducting enquiries in this house and the neighbouring ones,' Chandler replied as the colour began to return to his face. 'I'm told that the poor bugger was in safe custody in Leman Street at one time.'

'Until Thursday,' Reid replied morosely, 'then she insisted on being let out and we had nothing to hold her on. She gave an address in Dorset Street; I'll get my men to enquire down there in due course. But until recently she was using a room in a doss house in George Yard and that's why we were holding her, believing that she knew something about the Tabram killing there on Bank Holiday weekend.'

'I've finished here,' Phillips advised them both. 'Get the body to the mortuary on the handcart and I'll have a better look at her around lunchtime. I have a full hospital round before that, given this latest cholera outbreak.'

'What are you going to tell Enright?' Chandler enquired.

Reid smirked. 'As little as possible, although he'll find out soon enough. I'll keep his nephew busy up here on the north side, probably in Dorset Street; I think Percy Enright's getting his information from him.'

'Sir,' a constable announced as he poked his head round the open rear door to the yard and tried not to look down toward the body at the side of the steps, 'the man who found the body's anxious to get off to his work. Do you want to talk to him before you leave?'

'I'm not sure I'll be leaving soon,' Reid replied, 'and I definitely won't be in need of breakfast after this. So yes, send him out here. I'll look after this end, Joe,' he advised Inspector Chandler, who muttered his thanks and undertook to locate and detain any other witnesses there might be.

By the time that the Spitalfields Church clock struck nine, Reid had conducted several interviews and was beginning to build a very confused picture, although the tangled accounts given by the witnesses tended to suggest that Annie Chapman had died at around five thirty.

The man who'd found the body — a carman called John Davies who lived at the lodgings at number 29 — had discovered it lying to the side of the rear steps shortly before 6 am, when he went out into the yard with the intention of using the outside privy. He'd run back down the ground floor passage that ran from the rear into the street at the front and alerted two other men who were passing and who had viewed the body in situ, before one of them contacted police at Commercial Street. It had been Inspector Chandler who'd called in the police surgeon and the ambulance and when advised of the identity of the deceased he'd sent a constable down to Leman Street to alert Reid.

The last one to see Annie alive, apart, obviously, from her killer, was a Mrs Long, who came forward when news of the atrocity ran like wildfire through her place of employment in Spitalfields Market and the address struck a chord in her recent memory. She insisted, under rigorous interrogation from Reid, that shortly before five thirty that morning, she'd had seen a man and woman on the pavement adjoining number 29.

Later that morning, with protestations of disgust and revulsion, she identified the woman in the mortuary as the one she had seen and she described the man who had been with her as 'foreign looking' and 'shabby genteel' in appearance, approximately forty years of age, only slightly taller than Annie and wearing a dark coat. Because the man's back had been towards Mrs Long, she hadn't seen his face, but she'd heard a snippet of conversation, in which the man enquired 'Will you?' and the woman had replied 'Yes'. Taking them for a street prostitute and her client she thought no more about it until she heard about the murder and went back into Hanbury Street and spoke to a constable. Various residents of number 29 had also shamefacedly admitted that the ground floor passage and rear yard of the premises were frequently used by prostitutes to conduct business with their clients, although no-one had heard any sound during that particular early morning.

However, a man called Albert Cadosch who lived next door at number 27 stated that shortly before 5.30 am he had been in the adjoining yard, on the other side of the fence, when he heard a voice saying 'No'. There was no particular urgency in the voice and he could not be certain whether it was that of a man or a woman, but a few moments later he had heard something fall against the other side of the fence. He had not thought to look over it, since he assumed that it had something to do with the packing case business that was being conducted from the adjoining yard and the fence was some six feet high. However, it was obvious that had he done so, he would have observed the killer about their grisly work.

HIS

Chapter Eleven

Jack reported for work at six o'clock on the Monday morning, his head still full of the wonderful memories of the previous day that had kept him from sleeping. Esther had not laughed at, or poured scorn on, his protestation of love and although she had not expressed any reciprocating sentiment, a tear had formed at the corner of her eye as she thanked him for what she had called 'the compliment' and had kissed him warmly on the lips. On the train journey back on the London, Tilbury and Southend line to Fenchurch Street, and then by connecting horse bus back into Spitalfields, the conversation had centred around Jack's family and particularly his sister Lucy, who Esther seemed to have taken a strong liking to.

Now Jack was brought sharply back to reality by the news, given to the entire day shift as they rostered on duty, that the body of Dark Annie Chapman had been found horribly mutilated in a back yard in Spitalfields, only a few streets away from where Esther lived. Jack was told that Inspector Reid had a special task for him and when he tapped on his half-open door, the man in question looked up.

'Have you heard?' Reid enquired.

'About Dark Annie, you mean?'

'Yes. Does your uncle know yet?'

'I've no idea, sir. I haven't seen him since I came on duty.'

'Well when you do, don't tell him. He'll find out soon enough and I want my report to reach the Yard before he finds out that, according to one of the witnesses, it was done by a prostitute's client.'

'That doesn't mean a guardsman though, does it, sir?'

Reid smiled back at him. 'Keep thinking like that, Jack — and try and persuade your uncle.'

'What are the papers saying?'

'They don't know yet, since we haven't informed them. No point in spreading needless panic when we believe that these victims were targeted for something they knew and that it wasn't just the work of a random lunatic.'

'I was told you had a job for me, sir.'

'Indeed yes and it's in connection with this horrible business. Although we believe that the victim had a close connection with that disreputable thieves' kitchen in George Yard, Annie gave us an address in Dorset Street, number 35. Get up there and start asking questions and report directly back to me — not your uncle, understand?'

'Understood, sir.'

'Very well. Since I imagine that you'll use the excuse to visit a certain party in George Street while you're up there, reassure her that she's not the next target.'

'Can I advise her who the next target is, sir?'

'If I knew, I'd tell you. Anyway, off you go.'

Two hours later, Jack was getting conflicting opinions as he interviewed those at 35 Dorset Street who had known Annie Chapman in the weeks leading to her death. Most of her fellow lodgers remembered a friendly, cheerful drunk, while the Superintendent of the lodging house was more critical of her.

'She caused trouble 'ere, sometimes,' Timothy Donovan advised him. 'She were in a stupid fight wi' another lodger over a bit o' soap in the kitchen, then she went missin' fer a week or so. Then she comes back 'ere bold as brass on the Friday afore she died, askin' fer 'er old room back. She'd obviously 'ad a few an' were none too sober on the second night, but she didn't 'ave the money fer 'er room fer the night — a measly bloody fourpence, mind you. Last I saw of 'er, she went out down the street ter sell 'er bonnet, what she reckoned were worth fourpence. If the truth were told, I reckon she were off 'awkin' 'er body fer the money, but yer shouldn't speak ill o' the dead, now should yer?'

'She were dead scared o' summat, though,' chipped in Amelia Palmer, a lodger who happened to be in the kitchen, washing a man's shirt in the sink.

'How do you mean?' Jack enquired.

'Just like I said,' Amelia insisted. 'From the time she come back ter the time she set off ter sell 'er bonnet, she were lookin' fearful every time someone come in the building, like she were expecting someone ter come an' get 'er. She were normally a cheery soul, but from Friday onwards she were quiet, broodin' about summat, an' dead scared ter go outside.'

'Thank you, you've both been most helpful,' Jack concluded as he closed his notebook and put his helmet back on. 'If you remember anything else, just call in at Leman Street police station and ask for me — Constable Enright. Or, if it's more convenient, Inspector Chandler at Commercial Street. Good day.'

There was no doubt in his mind where he had to go next. The brutal murder of Annie Chapman was big news all over Spitalfields and it was unlikely that Esther wouldn't have heard about it from her fellow lodgers. She may not have associated the Annie Chapman who'd been murdered with the 'Dark Annie' she'd located in George Yard, but any excuse would do in Jack's book and George Street was only a few streets away.

'I 'opes yer spendin' yer time lookin' fer that bloke what did that 'orrible murder up the road there,' Sadie Thompson admonished him as he walked into the kitchen at Esther's lodgings, 'instead o' loungin' around 'ere drinkin' tea.'

'Actually, I'm here in connection with that,' Jack assured her. 'Is Miss Jacobs available for a few questions?'

'I'll go an' get 'er fer yer,' Sadie offered and Jack stood by the sink, notebook open as if he was there on official business, until he heard Esther's light footfall in the passageway and smiled warmly as she stepped into the kitchen, looked behind her, then rushed into Jack's arms, kissing him several times on the lips before taking a seat and straightening her hair, just as Mrs Thompson came back into the kitchen, as if to chaperone proceedings, before announcing that she needed 'ter spend a penny' in the outside privy, leaving them alone.

'You heard about the murder in Hanbury Street?' Jack enquired.

'Who hasn't?' Esther replied. 'It's the talk of the neighbourhood.'

'It was Dark Annie,' Jack advised her.

Esther's hand flew to her mouth and she stared back at him in horror. 'That can't just be coincidence, can it?' she insisted. 'First Polly Nichols, now Dark Annie. Both of them were women the police wanted to speak to about the guardsman and both of them have been done away with. But what was Annie doing in Hanbury Street, when she had a room in George Yard?'

'She had lodgings in Dorset Street as well,' Jack disclosed, 'and it seems that she went back to them two nights before she died. But she didn't have the money to pay for her bed the night she died, so she went back out on the street to get it. She was intending to sell either her bonnet or herself and she must have met the man who did it in the course of wandering the street.'

'The man?' Esther echoed. 'You mean the guardsman?'

Jack nodded. 'Even Inspector Reid believes it may have been him, posing as a customer. I read a description of the injuries on the body and believe me, whoever did that meant it and was very handy with something sharp.'

Esther shuddered and looked Jack directly in the eye. 'Do you think Polly suspects me of investigating her? Could I be the guardsman's next target?'

'I really don't think you need be alarmed,' Jack advised her, 'but best stay in your room until we get more information and hopefully catch the man responsible.'

'I hardly ever go out anyway,' Esther advised him, before breaking into a seductive smile and adding, 'except on Sundays, with a man who says he might be in love with me.'

'I am, believe me,' Jack reassured her, 'and you'll be in no danger walking out with me, even if I'm not in uniform, but it might be better if we go somewhere other than the local church yard.'

'Like Barking, you mean?'

'Possibly, although we might consider going up west or something. Please don't cancel our Sunday meetings, Esther — they mean so much to me.'

Esther got up, walked round the table and threw her arms around Jack before kissing him, then leaning back slightly in order to look him in the eye. 'Darling Jack, nothing would stop me spending Sunday afternoons with the man I think I may be in love with as well.'

Chapter Twelve

Edmund Reid seemed to be making a habit out of attending inquests. These last two had been conducted by the coroner for South East Middlesex, Wynne Baxter, and Reid was slowly losing ground in his efforts to persuade Scotland Yard that he had the matter well in hand and that the person behind it all was an army man.

First had been the inquest into the death in Bucks Row of Polly Nichols, which had been conducted over four separate days, by the last of which — on 22nd September — the coroner was painfully aware that he was also halfway through the inquest into the butchering of Annie Chapman in Hanbury Street. His summing up at the first inquest was heavily influenced by the evidence that had begun to emerge during the second, with a separate jury, and his words — faithfully recorded by journalists and published the following day — were the first to alert the general public to the possibility that a dangerous lunatic might be at work and still at large. As he advised his first jury:

'It seems astonishing at first thought that the culprit should have escaped detection, for there must surely have been marks of blood about his person. If, however, blood was principally on his hands, the presence of so many slaughter houses in the neighbourhood would make the frequenters of this spot familiar with blood-stained clothes and hands and his appearance might in that way have failed to attract attention while he passed from Bucks Row in the twilight into Whitechapel Road and was lost sight of in the morning's market traffic.'

He then drew attention to the fact that this was the third of four murders in the past five months, in which, 'All four victims were women of middle age, all were married, and had lived apart from their husbands in consequences of intemperate habits and were at the time of their death leading an irregular life and eking out a miserable and precarious existence in common lodging houses.'

Edmund Reid ground his teeth in silent exasperation as he listened to this last comment. As far as he was concerned, the death of Polly Nichols had been only the second in a series of three, because Emma Smith, who had been attacked in April of that year, had clearly advised those attending her in the hospital to which she had been taken that her attackers had been a gang of pimps out to teach her a lesson. This made Martha Tabram the first and Polly Nichols the second; furthermore, the evidence was not yet fully in on the Annie Chapman matter and the Coroner had no business spreading alarm and despondency with his speculation about a homicidal maniac on the loose, one who could surreptitiously creep up on his victims, silently hack them to pieces and then disappear like an early morning mist.

Baxter even had the audacity to openly link the last two — Nichols and Chapman — before either jury had returned a verdict, concluding; 'I suggest to you as a possibility that these two women may have been murdered by the same man with the same object and that in the case of Nichols the wretch was disturbed before he had accomplished his object and having failed in the open street he tries again, within a week of his failure, in a more secluded place.'

Little wonder that the jury, after only the briefest of consultations, had returned a verdict of 'wilful murder by a person or persons unknown.'

'There you go, Inspector,' Sergeant Enright gloated as they left the public seats, 'we're dealing with a deranged madman, as I shall advise the Yard.'

'I've already submitted my report on the Chapman killing,' Reid advised him, 'and I've left them in no doubt that it was the work of a blood-thirsty guardsman. I intend to commandeer the records from Wellington Barracks, to identify those who were not on duty on the relevant nights.'

'You'll need the Yard's authority for that, which you won't get,' Enright replied without relaxing the smirk. 'You heard the coroner's conclusion as clearly as I did. The person responsible is a clever lunatic and almost certainly has medical skills. A man with skills like that wouldn't have taken the Queen's shilling.'

'We'll see,' Reid muttered as he sidled his way down between the rows of seats.

Reid was even more incensed when he received the official post-mortem report from Dr Phillips, ahead of the inquest into the death of Annie Chapman, at which it would be delivered to the gentlemen of the press with their sharpened pencils and their noses for screaming headlines. George Bagster Phillips was an experienced police surgeon whose medical opinions tended to be received like the Holy Grail. He had concluded that: 'Obviously the work was that of an expert — of one, at least, who had such knowledge of anatomical or pathological examinations as to be enabled to secure the pelvic organs with one sweep of the knife, which must therefore have been at least five or six inches in length, probably more. The appearance of the cuts confirmed me in the opinion that the instrument, like the one which divided the neck, had been of a very sharp character. The mode in which the knife had been used seemed to indicate great anatomical knowledge.'

On the final day of the Annie Chapman inquest Dr Phillips, in answer to specific questions from the coroner, ruled out the use of a bayonet to inflict the injuries he had examined on the corpse of the deceased, thus further distancing any connection between that murder and that of Martha Tabram and insisted that the weapon used would not even be likely to be found among post-mortem medical implements. He also ruled out any knife used in the leather trades, on the ground that they would not be long enough and speculated that the victim's throat had been cut as the first action, thereby rendering Annie unconscious, if not instantly dead, before the other gruesome incisions were made and the uterus and upper vagina were completely removed and not found among the assorted viscera left lying on the victim's shoulder.

As if determined to give the press all the stomach-churning ammunition they needed, Coroner Baxter asked Phillips how long such a grisly process would have taken, to which Phillips replied, 'I think I can guide you by saying that I myself could not have performed all the injuries I saw on that woman, even without a struggle, in under a quarter of an hour. If I had done it in a deliberate way, such as would fall to the duties of a surgeon, it would probably have taken me the best part of an hour. The whole inference seems to me that the operation was performed to enable the perpetrator to obtain possession of these parts of the body.'

In his summary to the jury, the coroner made much of the fact that the killer could not have been aware of how many people were living in the house that went with the yard of 29 Hanbury Street, and the hours which they kept, but that he had nevertheless committed a series of savage surgical outrages on the body of a woman he had enticed into the yard on the pretence of requiring her sexual services. He went on to emphasise that the sexual organs that had been removed might have been the entire object of the offender's deranged actions, given that there was a ready market for such things in medical schools — indeed, the person responsible might be attending just such an establishment.

His eyes firmly fixed on Reid, in the third row from the front of the packed hall, the coroner added, 'Surely, it is not too much even yet to hope that the ingenuity of our detective force will succeed in unearthing this monster. It is not as if there were no clue to the character of the criminal or the cause of his crime. His object is clearly divulged. His anatomical skill carries him out of the category of a common criminal, for his knowledge could only have been obtained by assisting at post-mortems, or by frequenting the post-mortem room … we should know that he was a foreigner of dark complexion, over forty years of age, a little taller than the deceased, of shabby genteel appearance, with a brown deer-stalker hat on his head and a dark coat on his back. If your views accord with mine, you will be of opinion that we are confronted with a murder of no ordinary character, committed not from jealously, revenge, or robbery, but from motives less adequate than the many which still disgrace our civilisation, mar our progress and blot the pages of our Christianity.'

The predictable verdict was yet another murder 'by a person or persons unknown', but Reid was convinced that the person behind it all was not unknown to him, if only his hands were left sufficiently free for him to prove it.

Perhaps inevitably, those with nothing else to occupy their minds began writing to the newspapers with their theories regarding the person responsible for the two latest outrages and the editors were encouraged to pen one gruesome article after another. The speculation ranged from a discharged wounded serviceman with a grudge, to a Jewish conspiracy to eliminate all the Gentiles from East London. Then there were those who were convinced that the person responsible was a surgeon with a 'down' on prostitutes as the result of contracting syphilis, which was known to lead, in its final manifestation, to insanity. But one letter in particular had raised the fear level in the back alleys of Whitechapel.

It had been sent to the Central News Agency in London and was published in the same edition of the dailies that featured the findings of the Annie Chapman coronial jury. It was from a man who was taunting the authorities over their inability to catch him, revelling in the thrill he got from what he called 'my funny little games' and promising to cut the ears from his next victim and send them to the police. He signed himself 'Jack the Ripper' and a name had now been given to the nightmare stalking the dark alleyways of gas-lit Whitechapel and Spitalfields.

'Seen the morning papers?' Percy Enright gloated as he walked into Reid's office without knocking and threw several national dailies onto his desk upside down, so that Reid could peruse them, if he hadn't already. Indeed he had and he was more than angrily aware of the two inch banner headlines advising the local populace of the 'deranged lunatic' on the loose, of the 'mad doctor in search of women's most intimate body parts' and of 'the seeming inability of the police of this city to catch a maniac who must have been covered from head to foot in the blood of his victims.'

'So where do you suggest that we look, now that your theories of a revengeful prostitute have been blown out of the water?' Enright demanded.

'We?' Reid demanded, the colour rising in his face.

'Are you rejecting the assistance of Scotland Yard?' Enright enquired.

'Of course not,' Reid replied through gritted teeth.

'Perhaps as well,' Enright smiled back unpleasantly, 'since I've sent for Abberline.'

'Was that really necessary?'

'I rather think so, given that two local divisions have come up with nothing at the present time,' Enright replied.

Chapter Thirteen

Esther threw another handful of corn from the bag that Jack held open in his lap and a cluster of appreciative pigeons bobbed and cooed around their feet on the bench in Lincoln's Inn Fields. Another Sunday, another session of hand-holding and another exchange of kisses, as the warm Autumn sun added to the glow of the occasion.

'Why didn't you tell me your real name's Jackson?' Esther enquired teasingly.

'Because it's embarrassing to my mind. And only my mother calls me that. Even Lucy calls me Jack, if she wants to keep in my good books.'

'How did she get on with that young man she was trying to attract that day we were there?'

'Very well, it would seem, although she's giving you all the credit, since the fool made a polite comment about her gown and that led to a more general conversation.'

'She's so beautiful, she surely shouldn't need to worry at all about attracting the right sort of young man.'

'A bit like you, you mean?' Jack smiled at her. 'I can't believe I'm the first young man you've ever walked out with.'

'Jack, use your intelligence,' Esther replied. 'I'm Jewish, I'm a seamstress by profession and I live in a common lodging house in Spitalfields. That's hardly likely to have them rushing to knock on my door, is it?'

'But all of those excuses you just gave don't explain why no-one has ever before spotted your beauty, inside and out.'

'Maybe no-one's ever looked,' Esher suggested. 'Maybe it took the eagle eye of a police constable to look beyond the prejudice — racial and social.'

'It certainly took the eagle eye of a Detective Sergeant from Scotland Yard,' Jack chuckled. 'It's a good job Uncle Percy's in his early fifties, else I'd have a serious rival there. Seems that he gave my mother a very glowing report about you.'

'Talking of Scotland Yard, it seems to me that the key to this entire business is to be found in George Yard. Martha was killed there on a night when Polly Nichols was in the company of Pearly Poll and Annie Chapman was known to stay there from time to time. Everything comes back to that dreadful doss house in there. We know that some sort of military man pays the rent for a room on the very landing where Martha was stabbed and two women who might have been able to give us a clue about what happened to Martha in there have been killed by someone who might have access to sharp weapons.'

Jack whistled quietly. 'You have a very tidy mind for this sort of thing; it's a pity we don't recruit women into the Metropolitan Police.'

'Who knows, if one day we get the vote, like some people are beginning to suggest we should, that might change. Then you'll have to look to your laurels, Jackson Enright.'

'Please don't call me Jackson!' he pleaded.

'I seem to recall that you told me that Annie Chapman had been staying at 35 Dorset Street just before she died.'

'So?'

'So — when Pearly Poll gave evidence at the inquest into Martha's death, that's the address she gave as well.'

'You mean that she and Annie once shared the same address?'

'Yes, except that it doesn't take us any further, does it? We can connect the two women at that doss house in George Yard as well and that's where Martha died and where Annie had been staying until two nights before she was murdered. Perhaps the same "military type" man that rents the room in George Yard is the killer?'

'I'm sure Inspector Reid will have thought of that.'

'I've no doubt he has,' Esther agreed, 'but does he have any plans to keep watch for the man when he next calls to pay the rent?'

'No idea, but I'll suggest it to him,' Jack replied eagerly. 'Or perhaps the senior Scotland Yard man when he comes down tomorrow. Inspector Reid's chewing his hat over that and he's blaming Uncle Percy.'

'Doesn't it make it awkward for you, having Percy for an uncle?'

'Not normally, but he and Inspector Reid have certainly got their bootlaces entangled over these latest murders. Never mind, the Inspector can't fault me for the way I carry out my duties and Uncle Percy has such a high opinion of you that he wouldn't do anything to prejudice my career advancement.'

'Why would your career advancement have anything to do with me?' Esther enquired.

Jack went bright red with embarrassment before suggesting that they catch the horse bus back to the East End.

'Not a day too soon, it would seem,' Inspector Fred Abberline observed sarcastically as he walked into Reid's office without knocking and seated himself without being invited to do so. Reid rose from behind his desk and offered the newcomer his chair.

'I suppose you'll be wanting the use of my office while you're here?' he enquired acidly.

Abberline smiled back reassuringly. 'I spent long enough behind that desk in the old days, when I used to run you ragged. Keep it for the time being, Edmund. I'm going to be kept pretty busy running between police stations for most of today anyway, by the sound of it.'

'One of them's in the City,' Reid reminded him. 'I've already been warned off that one by the City Police Commissioner.'

'No doubt you have,' Abberline observed, 'but Sir Charles has cleared the way for me and they're expecting me down there while we stand here wasting time. I'll leave you and Percy Enright to investigate the one on your patch, then report to me. Both of you together, that is — I'm getting tired of separate memos from each of you, complaining about the other.'

They were dealing with what the evening papers would screamingly announce as a 'doubt event'. There had been two murders the previous night which, although little more than a ten minute walk apart, involved two separate police organisations. The one to which Fred Abberline was heading, with the unarguable authority of Metropolitan Police Commissioner Sir Charles Warren behind him, was in Mitre Square, only a few yards inside the territory of the City of London Police, traditionally independent of the Metropolitan Police within its one square mile of jurisdiction and fiercely protective of that independence. The second, to which, ironically, Reid would have further to walk than Abberline, was in Berner Street and the link between the two murder sites was the Commercial Road, heavy with pedestrians and traffic even in the early hours of the morning. If these two murders were the work of the same person, they had been very lucky not to get caught.

As Abberline passed through the token cordon of uniformed constables of the City Police at the Church Passage entrance to Mitre Square, he was met by Inspector Collard of the City CID and escorted to the place where the body had first been found, at around fifteen minutes to two that morning.

'We've obviously had the unfortunate wretch removed to the mortuary, at the request of Dr Brown, who first attended,' Collard advised him. 'It was a woman in her forties, very badly mutilated, and when we realised the similarity between this one and the one you men had in Spitalfields recently, my boss contacted yours.'

'Any witnesses?' Abberline enquired curtly.

'Several of our constables were on beat duty around the area at the time, but they neither saw nor heard anything, it seems. The body was discovered by Constable Watkins, who's seated in the gutter there, taking a rest. He was supposed to have come off night shift several hours ago, but I asked him to remain for long enough to talk to you, so if you'd be so good as to start with him, he can go home. He's badly shaken, I'm afraid.'

'Who's that civilian standing with that other constable?' Abberline enquired.

'A man called Lawende, who claims that he saw the victim standing talking to a man at the entrance to the passage you just came through.'

'I'll take him first,' Abberline insisted. 'Your constable will have to wait.'

By the middle of the morning, Abberline had pieced together a sorry tale of missed opportunities. It seemed that a mere ten minutes had elapsed between Constable Watkins' first sweep through Mitre Square, at 1.30 am, seeking among other things to flush prostitutes and their clients out of the convenient alcoves and doorways in the Square and his discovery of the body at 1.40 am. She was lying in a grotesque pose in one of the darkest parts of the Square, her skirts up around her waist, her stomach ripped open and her throat cut. Watkins had sounded the alarm and the police surgeon had been summoned. Watkins was adamant that he had seen and heard nothing, but the civilian witness Lawende proved more helpful.

He'd been leaving a club in Duke Street at 1.30 am when he had noticed a man and a woman at the entrance to Church Passage, which led into Mitre Square. He took the woman to be a prostitute, to judge by her generally dishevelled appearance and the man with her he described as being 'rather rough and shabby'. He was aged in his thirties, approximately five feet seven inches tall, of medium build with a fair moustache. He was wearing a loose-fitting 'pepper and salt' jacket and a grey peaked cap, with a 'reddish' scarf knotted around his neck. His overall appearance was that of a sailor and Abberline made a sour mental note that he would be obliged to make enquiries at the docks in due course, since the newspapers would no doubt carry accounts of an insane merchant seaman running amok once his vessel had tied up.

He was bracing himself to attend at the mortuary when he received a serious distraction. A police wagon pulled up in Duke Street and out stepped Sir Charles Warren.

'You might have waited for me, Abberline,' Warren declared, red in the face. 'I left not long after you and I've spent the past few hours in Goulston Street, a couple of streets up from here and clearly on our territory. One of our constables found a piece torn from an apron in a tenement up there and someone had written an anti-Jewish slogan on the wall above it. I ordered its removal before it caused a riot. Just to let you know, since I'm going back up to Whitehall without delay — the Home Secretary wants an urgent report before things get out of hand. Get me all you can on both murders and cable me the essential details before I leave for the day. Good day to you.'

Abberline sighed and went back to the matter in hand. Inspector Collard was still inside Mitre Square, which had filled with gawping spectators once the police had reopened access to it and Abberline was still in need of even basic information.

'Do we know who the victim is yet?' he enquired.

Collard inclined his head from side to side in a gesture of uncertainty. 'Not yet, but we found a pawn ticket in her possession in the name of Jane Kelly, with an address in Spitalfields, so you might want to send someone off to the pawnbroker.'

'That's my patch, isn't it?'

'Your patch, but our body. I'll let you know when we have something more positive.'

Abberline snorted derisively and headed for the mortuary.

Meanwhile, Reid and Percy Enright were surrounded by far too much information in nearby Berner Street. In Dutfield's Yard, which contained the club premises of the International Working Mens' Educational Society, they were surrounded by members who had been in the club in the early hours of that morning and were now clamouring to go home and get on with their lives, but were being sternly instructed to remain where they were until they had given statements.

The reason for all this was the discovery, at approximately 1 am, of a woman's body in the entrance to the yard. It had been found by a man returning to the yard in a cart pulled by a pony, which had shied when startled by the presence of the body in the open gateway. Her throat had been cut, but there were no other obvious injuries and Dr Phillips would later contrast the simplicity of these injuries with the more complex ones he had identified weeks earlier on Annie Chapman.

The victim was rapidly identified as 'Long Liz', a local prostitute whose real name was Elizabeth Stride, but who was believed to have been Swedish by birth. She was a regular at various public houses in the area and Berner Street was very much on her 'beat', where she would often be seen offering herself to men as they passed by where she would lounge suggestively in doorways, until their more lawful occupiers ordered her off.

Reid and Enright agreed with each other for once, in concluding that the man with the pony and cart — Louis Diemschutz — had almost certainly interrupted the final moments of this latest victim and that the assailant had made good their escape either by leaping the back fence of the yard, or slinking away under the cover of darkness as Diemschutz ran into the neighbouring club for assistance. The members of the club who had been detained until well into daylight hours were eventually allowed to leave after assuring either Reid or Enright that they had seen and heard nothing, given that songs were being sung within the club at the time of the discovery. When Reid made enquiry regarding the arrangements for the post-mortem, he was advised that this was being delayed because Dr Phillips had been called in by City Police Surgeon Dr Brown, given his previous experience of examining the body of Annie Chapman.

Reid found Abberline standing morosely alongside the two

doctors as they surveyed the as yet unidentified remains from Mitre Square.

'If this is the work of the same man who did for Annie Chapman,' Phillips observed, 'then he must have been well gone in liquor. Annie Chapman was anatomised with a precision that was almost clinical, whereas this one's simply been butchered.'

'The left kidney's missing,' Brown pointed out, 'and even I would have experienced considerable difficulty in removing that in almost total darkness, even though I know where to find it. Are you suggesting that a mere amateur got lucky?'

'He only took half the womb, though,' Phillips pointed out. 'He went in through the middle and slashed out the top half like he was scooping out a melon. If you or I were attempting that, would we not instead make a circular incision and remove the cervix while leaving the vagina intact? And how do you explain the facial lacerations? And all in the space of ten minutes, according to the witnesses?'

'Where are the clothes?' Abberline enquired.

'Over there, on that table,' he was advised. He walked across, carrying the piece of torn and blood-soaked apron he had been handed at Goulston Street and matched it exactly to the piece missing from the clothing removed from their nameless victim.

'Our well-butchered lady may have been in Goulston Street at some time prior to her death,' he observed.

'At least, part of her apron was,' Reid corrected him. 'It may well be that our killer dropped it on his way back from either Berner Street or Mitre Square.'

'We don't even know if the two deaths are connected,' Abberline reminded him. 'Or what order they occurred in.'

'I'm no police officer,' Phillips reminded him sardonically, 'but if the woman in the club yard died at 1 am and —

according to Brown here — this woman was done in at least half an hour later, doesn't that suggest the order of service?'

'Perhaps,' Reid conceded, 'but I need to add in the remaining information that Sergeant Enright was left there to collect.'

The sun was setting through the side window of Reid's first floor office as he and Enright began pooling what they had got, ahead of the return of Abberline, who had bravely undertaken to remain for the remainder of the post-mortem on the Mitre Square corpse. Enright was quite pleased with himself.

'I managed to locate several witnesses to Stride's last known movements,' he smiled, 'and the most promising is a Constable Smith, who saw a woman answering her description in Berner Street, opposite the club, with a man in tow. The man is described as 28 years old, wearing a dark coat and a hard deerstalker hat. He was carrying a parcel approximately 6 inches high and 18 inches in length, wrapped in newspaper. It could, of course, have been yesterday's fish, but my bet is that it was a knife.'

'When was this?' Reid enquired.

'About 12.30 in the morning, according to Smith.'

'We'll have to wait for Abberline and see if he has any matching description,' Reid conceded, 'but I'm slowly abandoning my original theory that the killer might be connected in some way with Pearly Poll.'

'Not before time,' Enright replied quietly. 'So what's next?'

'Find out all you can from that pawnbroker. I'd like to at least know the identity of those pathetic remains in the City mortuary.'

Chapter Fourteen

Working closely together, uncle and nephew finally had a name for the Mitre Square corpse. Percy Enright had been set the task of identifying her and had been allowed, at his request, to take Jack with him, 'in order to acquaint himself with the finer points of detective work.' Since Reid still suspected that Jack would pass on anything he discovered to Scotland Yard anyway, via his uncle, he had agreed and the two men had begun with the pawnbroker at whose premises a lady giving the name Jane Kelly had pawned a pair of boots two days previously.

The pawnbroker had given them an address of Cooney's Lodging House in Flower and Dean Street that 'Jane Kelly' had given as her home address. There was only one other person called Kelly living there and he initially tried to deny any knowledge of the lady, until the doss house Superintendant 'peached' on him by informing an insistent Percy Enright that a woman calling herself 'Mrs Jane Kelly' shared the room occupied by her presumed husband John. John Kelly had finally broken down when confronted with the mangled remains at the mortuary and had tearfully advised them that the lady's real name had been Catherine Eddowes, although she was believed to have once been married to a man named Conway. She had also, he advised them, been 'a hopeless pisspot' and something of an embarrassment to him, as the result of which he was seriously considering throwing her out on her ear if she didn't start bringing in some money towards the rent.

Catherine had disappeared on the day before her death, claiming that she was journeying to Bermondsey to borrow money from her daughter. She may well have succeeded, it seems, since Kelly had heard a rumour — subsequently confirmed — to the effect that Catherine had been picked up by police, hopelessly drunk in Aldgate High Street and held at Bishopsgate Police Station until she was sufficiently sober to be released at one o'clock in the morning.

Her movements during the final half hour of her life were a mystery, since her most direct route home would have been straight through Aldgate and left up Commercial Street. Instead she had for some reason or other wandered into Duke Street, perhaps in search of licensed premises that might still be open and it was there that she had been seen with the man believed to have been her killer. But the journey from Bishopsgate to Duke Street should not have taken her more than ten minutes, so where had she been in the meantime? She had no money on her body, so had she perhaps been robbed?

It was while John Kelly was reminiscing tearfully about his seven happy years with Catherine that something dropped out that made Jack prick up his ears. He was the one taking notes while Uncle Percy was asking the questions and Kelly had mentioned that apart from her fondness for too much alcohol, Catherine had been a friendly, helpful sort of woman who would go out of her way to help anyone, 'even girls what gets inter trouble.'

'What did you mean by that?' Jack enquired.

'Well, she knew this woman what could get rid o' babies what wasn't wanted, if yer get me drift an' she were always ready ter make the necessary introductions.'

'You mean that Catherine knew an abortionist?' Jack persevered.

'Yeah, if that's what yer calls 'em,' Kelly agreed.

'Do you happen to know where this woman operated from?' Jack enquired with a warning glance at his uncle.

'Dunno exactly, an' I wouldn't want ter get anybody in trouble wi' you lot,' Kelly replied, 'but I did once 'ear Kate tell someone — a woman called Kelly, funny enough — that it were somewhere down Whitechapel 'Igh Street.'

'Do you have an address for this Kelly woman?' Percy enquired.

Kelly shrugged his shoulders. 'Somewhere off Dorset Street, as far as I were told, not that it were any o' my business. She only come 'ere the once, ter ask Kate about the woman what did abortions an' she weren't the only one. I only remember 'er on account've us 'avin' the same name — she were called Mary Kelly — but as far as I could tell we weren't related. I 'ope not anyroad, since they reckon she's the biggest tottie in Dorset Street, an' *that's* sayin' summat. Kelly's a pretty common name around 'ere an' she were proper Irish, not like me, born an' bred in Bow.'

'I think that concludes our questions, Mr Kelly,' Percy advised him. 'We'll leave you in peace now, to grieve over your loss. I'll be sure to let you know when the inquest's to be held.'

'What did you make of that?' Jack enquired as they made their way down Brick Lane on their way back to Leman Street.

'Seemed an honest enough cove,' Percy replied, 'but what was the relevance of those questions about an abortionist? You still trying to keep in Reid's good books, with his crackpot theory about Pearly Poll?'

'It means another possible link between the lady in question and the series of murders,' Jack advised him. 'We think that Poll runs her baby murdering business from George Yard,

107

which is just off Whitechapel High Street. If this latest victim — Catherine Eddowes, as we now know her to be — was acting as some sort of pimp for Poll's abortion business, then she may have been another one who Poll wanted silenced by her tame lunatic.'

'Take my advice, young Jack,' Percy replied, 'never form a firm opinion too early in a case and then try to make the evidence fit your theory. Keep an open mind and store every little bit of information you get, until the conclusion's inescapable. Like my conclusion that the young lady heading towards us is made just for you.'

Even from a distance Jack had no difficulty in identifying the most important young lady in the world to him, but it wasn't until they were barely ten yards away from her that she looked up from the ground beneath her feet, gave a slight start, then broke into a beaming smile.

'Jack! And Mr Enright! What brings you up this way?'

'What else?' Jack replied. 'There's been another murder — Aldgate way this time, so don't worry — but the victim lived just up the road behind us and we've been questioning her man. And now tell us what you're doing heading that way.'

'I'm on my way to Lamb Street, with my latest completed work in this holdall, and hopefully I'll be bringing some new work back with me. I prefer to walk up Brick Lane, rather than Commercial Street, which is always much dustier and noisier, but if I'd gone the other way I'd have missed you completely. I hope we're still on for Sunday?'

'Of course we are,' Jack grinned back. 'We can decide where to go when I pick you up.'

'Keep him safe, won't you Percy?' Esther smiled before walking on.

'She called me Percy, like she was already family!' the older man mused out loud, his face radiant with the experience. 'Jack, my boy, have you asked her to marry you yet?'

'What, on a mere constable's wage?' Jack chortled back. 'I'd need to be a sergeant at least before I could think of even broaching the subject.'

'By which time someone else might have swept her up,' Percy replied. 'I married your Aunt Beattie when I was only a constable and she won't wait for ever — not a beautiful young thing like that.'

'But then there's Mother,' Jack objected as they crossed Montague Road and entered Osbourne Street.

'Leave your mother to me,' Percy replied with a grin. 'I think, to judge by her latest letter, that she's very pleased that you've finally found someone to make you happy. She was beginning to wonder about you.'

'Wonder what?'

'Never you mind. But Constance has always judged people by what they are and not who they are. Esther's a very honest upright young lady who just happens to be living in reduced circumstances.'

'Too reduced for Mother to approve, surely?'

'Your mother's very particular, Jack, but she's no snob. So why don't you take Esther back to Barking next Sunday and I'll invite myself up as well? Beattie's off to her sister's in Clacton for some sea air to clear her lungs and I haven't had a decent meal for days.'

'At least we'll be getting out of this awful place for a few hours,' Jack observed as they dodged between the wagons in order to cross Whitechapel Road.

'The awful place in which you hope to make it to sergeant, you mean?' Percy teased him as he joined him on the far pavement.

Chapter Fifteen

'We need to find this maniac without delay,' Abberline insisted as he sat with Edmund Reid and Percy Enright in Reid's office, considering their next move. They had flooded the area with extra men, and there was hardly a street corner or alleyway entrance in the whole of Whitechapel and Spitalfields that didn't have a police officer standing with a whistle, lantern and truncheon from dusk until dawn, but the people were still demanding that the person responsible for the outrages be identified and removed from the streets.

The atmosphere in those streets was so fearful and poisonous that the mere suggestion that some innocent passer-by fitted the general description of the lunatic still at large was likely to result in him being either torn apart by the mob, or strung up from a lamp post by locally self-appointed vigilantes. Also under suspicion were Jews of any age or gender, anyone such as a cobbler or slaughterman who worked with knives and even 'toffs' who occasionally put in an appearance from the safety of a cab.

The impetus for this urgent meeting was another postcard from the man calling himself 'Jack the Ripper' that had been sent to the Central News Agency the day after 'the double event'. In it, the writer had made reference to the fact that he had just carried out what he called a 'double event' and that 'number one squealed a bit couldn't finish straight off, had not the time to get ears for police.'

'Do you believe it's genuine?' Reid enquired. 'Or did some joker have access to an early edition of the papers?'

'Use your brains, Edmund,' Abberline demanded. 'He could have learned about "the double event" that way, but how was he to know that he hadn't managed to get the ears that he promised to send us on his next job? Catherine Eddowes had part of one ear cut off, as if he'd at least tried, but been disturbed, perhaps by the City bobby who found the body.'

'Is the handwriting the same on both letters?' Percy enquired.

'Apparently,' Abberline replied.

'So what do you suggest we do next?' Reid enquired in a tone of impending defeat.

'You're the local man — any brilliant ideas?' Abberline challenged him.

Percy thought for a moment before making his own suggestion. 'Most importantly, we have to be seen to be doing something. Constable Enright mentioned that there may be some link with a doss house in George Yard, whose Superintendent Reid hauled in here and grilled, with no outcome.'

'That's right,' Reid growled, 'a woman called Ada Bushell, who seemed highly amused by the prospect of being done for "living off". Nothing would give me greater pleasure than to run her in for anything we can stick on her.'

'What's this got to do with our Ripper?' Abberline grumbled.

'We don't know unless we probe deeper, do we?' Reid countered. 'There was a murder in there a few weeks back, which I believe was the start of the slashings conducted by this monster and since then we've managed to connect the remaining victims with the same doss house.'

'Even this latest one?'

'The Mitre Square one, anyway. There's believed to be an abortion factory conducted in George Yard Buildings and from what Sergeant Enright here was able to discover,

Catherine Eddowes was acting as some sort of pimp or agent for the woman we believe to be the abortionist.'

'It was my nephew Jack who got us that information — don't forget him,' Percy reminded the other two.

'We're not likely to while you're around,' Reid grumbled.

'What about the first murder?' Abberline enquired. 'The one before Catherine Eddowes — the one that was interrupted, before he went on to the second one.'

'We don't know for certain that the murders occurred in that order,' Reid objected. 'This latest letter from the lunatic calling himself "Jack the Ripper" referred to the attempt to remove Catherine Eddowes' ears as "number one". We only know the times when the bodies were discovered; for all we know, the City bobby missed Eddowes' corpse the first or second time round the block. Or perhaps he wasn't patrolling his beat at all — just lounging in a doorway, having a smoke.'

'I hope you don't suggest that to anyone outside this room,' Abberline warned him. 'We're having a hard enough job getting their co-operation as it is. But we're getting away from the original point; what do you have in mind regarding this abortion place you mentioned? And you didn't answer my question about any link between the victim Stride and that place.'

'None at all that we know of at this stage,' Reid admitted. 'But so far as concerns the room in George Yard, we did manage to get out of Ada Bushell the fact that the rent's paid monthly in advance, on the same day each month, by someone she described as "a military type of gent". Coincidentally, a guardsman was suspected of that first murder, on the first floor landing in there.'

'Did this Ada woman say on what day of the month the rent was paid?' Enright enquired, his face alight with interest.

'The seventh, from memory,' Reid replied, 'but I can always check back through my notes. Why?'

Enright and Abberline exchanged looks and it was Abberline who spoke for them both. 'If I understand where Percy's thoughts are leading, we could try a stake-out on rent day.'

'I hardly think that anyone engaged in criminal activity in that yard is likely to turn up to make a rental payment when the place is crawling with uniformed police,' Reid objected.

'Precisely,' Abberline agreed, 'but at the Yard we regularly engage in this sort of "under-cover" activity, as we call it. How do you think we busted that network of thieves in the Albert Dock a few months ago? Or that arsonist in Highgate? We used our own men, in plain clothes of course, posing as anything other than police officers. In the docks take-down they'd been working as wharfingers for several weeks and in the Highgate case they posed as various types of street vendor.'

'We're not that far behind the times down here in the slums,' Reid protested. 'We often catch pickpockets by mingling with large crowds dressed in our ordinary clothes.'

'Then you get the general idea,' Abberline pointed out. 'Since Percy here has more regular experience of how it's done, we'll leave it to him. On the seventh, which is less than a week away, he takes a team of your constables, dressed in mufti, into this yard and they wait for the military gentleman to pay his rent, then haul him in and tip him upside down for information.'

'I imagine that one of the constables he wishes to take will be his own nephew?' Reid enquired sarcastically.

Percy nodded. 'And not just him. His lady friend as well, if she's agreeable.'

Chapter Sixteen

'This is turnin' inter a regular police station an' no mistake,' Sadie Thompson complained as Percy, Jack and Esther sat around the small kitchen table at 19 George Street that somehow seemed too prosaic for the plan they were hatching.

'This is police business, missus,' Percy advised her. 'Haven't you got any housework you could be getting on with?'

'Are you suggestin' that this 'ouse is filthy?' Sadie demanded, hand on hips. 'If so, I'll 'ave yer know that there's a waitin' list fer a room in 'ere.'

'And we're waiting to make use of this room on official police business,' Percy insisted.

Sadie flounced out, leaving Esther to make tea, while Percy resumed the conversation with Jack that had been interrupted by Sadie's expressions of disapproval.

'You and your fellow constables hang around the entrance to the Yard, dressed in your everyday clothes rather than your police uniforms, posing as hawkers or costermongers, or whatever. It shouldn't be difficult to spot a military man among the riff-raff that normally congregate in places like that and when you spot him, you hang on to him and one of you comes inside the public house next door — what's it called again? — and alerts me. I'll do the arrest and then we hand him over to Inspector Reid.'

'Why do you need Esther?' Jack enquired.

'I was about to ask the same question,' Esther added, as she placed the cups down on the table. 'Do you want me to pose as a flower seller or something?'

'No,' Percy replied with a smile. 'I want you inside the pub with me. I'll be less conspicuous as a man enjoying a quiet drink with his daughter and once I get the tip-off that our quarry's been apprehended, you can come home.'

'I don't want her exposed to any danger,' Jack insisted.

'Very touching and gallant,' Esther replied somewhat sourly, 'but I'm perfectly capable of looking after myself.'

'When was the last pub fight you were in?' Jack countered and Esther wrinkled her face in displeasure.

'There'll be none of that,' Percy advised them both, 'and there'll be plenty of bobbies around to break up any violent reaction to the arrest. We'll do it in the Yard itself, so as to reduce the size of the audience. First sign of a police presence and in my experience they'll scatter.'

Two days later Percy and Esther made their way into the snug bar of the White Hart, where Percy ordered two glasses of beer. The two women who sat in the corner, clearly hoping for early customers to judge by their loud clothing, looked disapprovingly at the potential competition from Esther before they concluded, by means of exchanged whispers, that she already had her 'fancy man' for the day.

'What shall we talk about?' Esther enquired nervously.

'The one thing we have in common, at this stage,' Percy replied. 'Jack.'

'I can't think of anyone I'd rather talk about,' Esther beamed back. 'Does he really like me, do you think?'

'I think it goes deeper than that,' Percy replied. 'I wouldn't be surprised if he asks you to marry him.'

Esther blushed and giggled at the same time, before her gaze dropped down to the table at which they were seated. 'That's rather leaping ahead, isn't it? We've never even begun to discuss that sort of thing and then there's his mother ...'

'You needn't worry about her being a snob or anything,' Percy reassured her. 'Once she's satisfied that you're right for Jack, she wouldn't care if you did sell flowers in the street, like you suggested as your pose today.'

'Jack says we're all going out to Barking again on Sunday. Is that right?'

'I'll certainly be going — and for lunch, what's more. The family cook does a wonderful Sunday roast and my wife's away at the moment. I never learned to cook, so it's chop house meals for me at the moment. If this stake-out goes on for too long, we might try one of those pies I saw on the counter out in the public bar there.'

'Do you think they'll catch this army type?' she enquired.

'Who knows? It's got to be worth a try, though, since there's definitely some funny business going on in that place, according to Inspector Reid.'

'You knew that my friend died in there?' Esther enquired. 'Martha Turner?'

'She was the first Ripper victim, according to the Inspector. But Inspector Abberline's not convinced. What are you staring at? If it's a military type, don't stare and give the game away.' Percy had seen Esther's eyes widen and as she looked hastily down at the table in discomfort and revulsion, he asked, 'Who is it?'

'Over at the other table. The big woman who's just joined those two totties who're obviously on the lookout for marks — it's Pearly Poll. Don't look round.'

Percy chuckled. 'You're talking to an experienced undercover police detective, remember? And don't *you* display any surprise at what I do next.' Without further warning, he took Esther's hand in his, leaned forward and planted a kiss on her cheek. 'I'm going outside to see if there's been any action,' he whispered while their faces were still close together. 'Does that side door to this bar lead directly into the Yard?'

'No idea,' Esther whispered back, 'but it's the door Pearly Poll came through.'

'Just wait here until I return,' Percy instructed her as he stood up and walked to the door, openly leering at Poll's two companions on his way out. He was no sooner out of the door than Poll came across the room and sat down in the seat he'd just vacated.

'That yer fancy man?' she enquired.

Esther blushed and looked down at the table. 'And what if he is?' she enquired.

'Just make sure yer don't charge 'im less than ten bob, if 'e wants yer fer the day,' Poll advised her. 'An' if yer doin' it casual, like me two friends over there, make sure that yer charges at least a bob a knob. Two bob lyin' down. Make the best money while yer still young an' fresh an' if yer lookin' ter make a regular livin' that way, I can put yer in the way o' regular business any time yer likes — I'm always in 'ere fer the night trade.'

Out in the alleyway, Percy Enright took out his purse, extracted a few coins and walked casually up to the boy shining shoes to one side of the narrow passageway. As he became the last one waiting, he put one of his boots onto the raised box and enquired, 'No sign of him yet? '

'No,' Jack replied. 'But Pearly Poll went in and out a few minutes ago, then she went into the pub next door.'

'She's in the snug,' Percy advised him. 'I'd better get back in there and keep an eye on your intended. Where are the others?'

'Constable Preedy's lying further up there, mumbling nonsense and pretending to be drunk. Constable Draycott's selling bootlaces near the front entrance to the White Hart and Constable Shanahan's the one cleaning that side window to the lodging house, for the first time in years to judge by the look of it.'

'Keep me posted,' Percy requested, then moved back into the snug bar. Pearly Poll vacated his seat with a curt, 'bin keepin' it warm fer yer,' and rejoined her companions in the corner, seating herself so that she could keep an eye on Esther and Percy.

'Poll thinks you're my gentleman friend,' Esther smiled up at him in what she hoped was a 'come on' look designed to dispel any suspicions that Poll might be entertaining. 'How's it going outside?'

'No sign of anyone except Pearly Poll, who went in and out of the doss house, according to Jack.'

'Maybe she was paying the rent on behalf of the military man.'

'I'm about to get up and leave and I suggest that you follow shortly after me, looking as much as you're capable like a prostitute following her mark out to the designated place of assignation. I think we're done here for the day.'

'I'm not about to leave just yet,' Esther replied conspiratorially. 'I'm beginning to get the taste for this police undercover work. What was the name of that woman Jack was telling me about — the one who may have made use of Pearly Poll's abortion service?'

'He was supposed to keep that information strictly for police officers,' Percy grumbled, as he thought back for a moment, before his trained memory kicked in. 'Kelly. Mary Kelly, why?'

'I think I can get you the evidence you need about Poll and her abortion business.'

'I don't know what you have in mind, but for God's sake be careful.'

Percy wandered off via the public bar with the slight suggestion of a drunken stagger.

Esther waited for a few more minutes, during which she fidgeted with a handkerchief which she took from the sleeve of her jacket and when she could tell with her lowered glance that she had Poll's full attention, she stifled a sob that a Drury Lane actress would have been proud of. Poll eased her bulk off her seat and wandered over.

'What's the matter, lovey? 'As yer fancy man left yer in the lurch?'

'In a manner of speaking,' Esther replied while feigning the choking back of a further sob. 'He's a married man and now that I'm in the family way he wants to stay with his wife. He's offered me ten pounds to get rid of the child inside me and I was too shy to ask you earlier if you'd be prepared to help me until I knew how much I could offer you.'

'What makes yer think I could 'elp yer?' Poll demanded.

'A woman I met at the market up near where I live. Mary Kelly? She told me that a woman called Pearly Poll could see me right, but she didn't know how much you'd require.'

'Mary Kelly, eh?' Poll replied. 'She the one what lives in a doss in Dorset Street?'

'No idea,' Esther replied. 'I just met her in Spitalfields Market when I took a giddy turn and she came to my assistance. Can you help me, for ten pounds?'

'Come back 'ere a week today and I'll see yer right,' Poll promised, then walked through the side door and into the alley that formed part of George Yard. She stared down towards the street exit, where Percy was talking to the young constable who'd been with that police inspector at the inquest into Martha's death, except today he wasn't wearing his uniform. With a dismissive smirk she turned and went back to the lodging house up the alleyway.

Chapter Seventeen

'You obviously still have the same cook,' Percy Enright smiled across at his sister-in-law Constance as he laid the spoon down on the plate with a sigh of satisfaction. 'The lamb was roasted to perfection and that apple tart was fit for the Queen.'

They were all seated around the dining table in the house in Church Lane, Barking, and had just completed the finest meal Esther could ever remember. Even her own mother's cooking had been, to put it politely, adequate and there was a limit to how often one could enjoy gefilte fish. She had amazed herself by how much she had managed to consume, given her normal diet of bread and cheese, but she was relieved that there were no more courses and that Alice was busily engaged in clearing the table.

'It was indeed delicious,' Esther complimented Constance from where she sat next to Percy, with Jack and Lucy across the table on either side of their mother, 'and thank you so much for inviting us.'

'I like to ensure that Jackson gets at least one good meal every so often,' Constance replied with a smile and a sidelong glance at her son, 'since I dread to think what rubbish he normally eats from those chop houses and pie shops in that dreadful East End. As for Percy, he's probably been eating the same unwholesome fare while Beattie's away, so I considered it my Christian duty to ensure that two members of my family were properly fed for once. Shall we take tea in the sitting room?'

'Actually,' Percy replied diplomatically, 'I rather feel the need for a walk around the garden after all that goodness. Would you care to join me, Jack?' he added in what sounded more like a command than a suggestion.

Jack murmured his assent, shot Esther a reassuring look and got up from the table. As he did so, Constance turned to Lucy and indicated with a jerk of her head that she should also make herself scarce. This left just Constance and Esther to walk through to the sitting room and take armchairs facing each other while Alice left off clearing the lunch table and fussed around the low table between them with the tea things.

Once Alice had bowed out again, Constance fixed Esther with a firm stare and opened up. 'Esther, would you be so good as to answer me a few questions?'

'Certainly,' Esther replied nervously, 'always assuming that I know the answers.'

'Oh, you'll know the answers to these questions, let me assure you,' Constance replied. 'First of all, would I be correct in stating that you are Jewish by birth?'

'Yes,' Esther confirmed apprehensively.

'And from where did your ancestors originate?'

'As far as I've been told, from somewhere called Lithuania. I believe it to be near Russia, but my father was only a young boy when they were forced to flee and he had little memory of the place where he was born.'

'But, despite his unfortunate background, he built up a successful business — cloth importation, as I recall you telling me during our last meeting.'

'That's right. Then he was killed, along with my mother, and the business had to be sold.'

'And you then went into garment manufacture?'

'Well, the people who sort of adopted me had such a business, yes.'

'And that is how you acquired your undoubted skills with needle and thread?'

'Yes.'

'And that is how you now earn your living?'

'Yes.'

'In short, you are a seamstress?'

'That's correct.'

'And from what I can gather from the little that I have been able to wheedle out of Jackson and his uncle, you are currently residing in a common lodging house in Spitalfields?'

'Yes, but it's one of the respectable ones,' Esther insisted, feeling more uncomfortable with each question.

'So, if you were to marry Jackson, you would enjoy a considerable improvement in material comfort and living conditions?'

Esther had finally reached the boundaries of the politeness to which she considered her hostess to be entitled. Her face set as she replied. 'First of all, you should know that your son has never once mentioned marriage, let alone proposed it to me. Secondly, be advised that were I to marry Jack it would be for love and not for material advancement. And finally, I am proud of who I am and who my parents were and I feel no shame in having survived for six years by my own hard work and skills, without resorting to thieving, drinking or hawking my body in the street as a common prostitute. So while I may not be good enough for your dear son, neither am I an adventuress or an imposter. I imagine that this concludes our conversation — would you like me to leave now?'

Constance's face broke into a wide smile as she shook her head. 'On the contrary, I wish you to marry Jackson. My questions were designed only to assess your honesty. It's obvious to anyone that you and Jackson are very deeply attached to each other and I simply wanted to protect him from being seduced by your beauty into making a totally inappropriate match, in which love came a very poor second to social ambition.'

Esther rose from her armchair, red in the face and glared down at Constance.

'Gratifying though it is to have passed the mother-in-law test, Jack has yet to ask for my hand in marriage. If — and when — he does, I shall be obliged to decline, in case there is any lingering doubt in his mind regarding the genuineness of my love for him, as there so obviously was in yours. Good day, Mrs Enright, and thank you once again for the lunch.'

She bustled out of the sitting room, down the hallway and through the kitchen, past a startled cook who was sitting with her feet up, enjoying a cup of tea with Alice. Once in the back garden Esther stormed up to where Jack stood talking with his uncle and demanded that Jack take her home.

'Why?' Jack demanded, completely nonplussed by the look on her face that he had never seen before.

'I'll tell you on the way home,' Esther advised him with grim determination. 'Or if you prefer, I'll take off by myself and leave you with your dear Mama.'

'Best go with her, Jack,' Percy advised him. 'A young lady like her might not be safe on a train alone, these days.'

It took Jack all his effort to keep up with Esther as she steamed down Church Lane with her head down, fighting back tears of anger, humiliation and disappointment.

'What on earth did Mother say to upset you?' he demanded.

'Ask her yourself!' Esther spat back.

'I can't, can I, since we're heading back into the City?'

'Just leave it alone,' she demanded.

'How can I leave it alone?' Jack protested. 'My mother has obviously said something that didn't agree with you and I need to know what it was, if we're to continue seeing each other.'

Esther stopped suddenly and glared angrily into Jack's face as the first tears broke free and rolled down her reddened cheeks. 'She more or less called me a whore on the make! A scheming hussy using her feminine charms to seduce her precious boy. A Jewish seamstress with ideas above her true station in life. Well, neither of you need worry on that score, believe me! See me safely home, then we're finished, Jack Enright!'

'I'm still not convinced that we've got these last two in the right order,' Reid complained to Percy Enright as they stood outside St. George's Vestry Hall, Cable Street, in which the Coroner for South East Middlesex, Wynne Baxter, who had presided over the inquests into the deaths of Polly Nichols and Annie Chapman, was about to do the same in respect of the death of Elizabeth Stride outside the club in Berner Street.

'Since Catherine Eddowes is a City case, Baxter has no authority over that, at least,' Enright observed, to which Reid snorted by way of reply.

'That won't stop the blabbering old fool playing to the gallery, inflaming the newspaper columnists and causing panic in the streets' he added. 'Anyway, best go in and do what we can to hose things down.'

He was to be bitterly justified in his gloomy prediction that the press would have a field day. It was October 1st, the first day of the inquest, and the evidence of the first few witnesses was formal and uncontroversial. It established the discovery of Stride's body in the gateway to the club, still warm, at approximately 1 am, and the fact that no-one had seen or heard anything. It was then realised that there had been no formal identification of the deceased and the inquest was adjourned until the following day.

On that second day, as he had been on the previous day, Reid was sitting with the coroner, assisting with the acquisition of evidence from the various witnesses, the third of whom tearfully confirmed that the remains she had viewed at the mortuary had been those of her sister, Elizabeth Stride, and that she had been leading a somewhat irregular life, prone to bouts of drunkenness and living from time to time with different men. Then it was the turn of Constable Lamb of 'H' Division, who had been called to the body when it was first discovered and who had sent for the police surgeon. The second day concluded with more witnesses who confirmed the deceased's irregular lifestyle in one doss house after another, her fondness for alcohol and the fact that she had lived with several men during her forty odd years. The most recent of these, Michael Kidney, became involved in a heated exchange with Reid when he criticised the inability of the police to take immediate steps to apprehend the offender, whose identity Kidney implied that he might know, although he obstinately declined to disclose it to the coroner.

It was day three before Dr Phillips was called to give his formal report, to the effect that cause of death was the cutting of the throat, which would have rendered the victim dead almost immediately. There were no other wounds on the body and in Dr Phillips's opinion the body had not been moved to where it had been found. Put succinctly, Elizabeth Stride had been attacked without warning, she had been pushed to the ground and her throat had been slashed where she lay, which was where she had been found. The fatal act would only have taken seconds and in response to a specific question from the coroner, Phillips testified that the severance of the carotid artery in this case was totally unlike like the similar outrage inflicted on Annie Chapman.

Here we go, Reid told himself. *The idiot's trying to tie all these together as the work of one man. Unfortunately, he may be right.*

The next witness seemed destined to prove precisely that. A local man, William Marshall, testified to having seen the deceased, some forty-five minutes prior to the estimated time of her death, across the road from the club talking to a middle aged man wearing a peaked cap 'something like what a sailor would wear.' He was about five feet six inches in height, rather stout in build and decently dressed. Marshall did not see his face and could not say whether or not he had any facial hair, or whether or not he was carrying anything. The couple were kissing from time to time and he heard the man tell the deceased: 'You would say anything but your prayers,' in reply to which the woman had laughed. Then, just to confuse matters, another police officer testified to having seen the same couple in precisely the same place, but testified that the man had been wearing a deerstalker hat and carrying a parcel approximately 18 inches long and 8 inches broad.

Reid was then called to testify to the course of the police enquiries which had led to the location of the witnesses who had testified, but had taken them no closer to identifying the offender. 'The investigation is still going on. Every endeavour is being made to arrest the assassin, but up to present without success,' he added.

It was 23rd October before the inquest was concluded and Wynne Baxter could not resist widening his concluding remarks to well outside the matter for the consideration of the jury when he concluded that: 'There was no skilful mutilation as in the cases of Nichols and Chapman and no unskilful injuries, as in the case in Mitre Square. This is possibly the work of an imitator; but there was the same skill exhibited in the way in which the victim had been entrapped and the injuries inflicted, so as to cause instant death and prevent blood from soiling the operator and the same daring defiance of immediate detection, which, unfortunately for the peace of the inhabitants and trade of the neighbourhood, has hitherto been only too successful. Speaking for myself, I am sorry that the time and attention which you, the jury, have given to the case has not produced a result that would be a perceptible relief to the metropolis — the detection of the criminal; but I am bound to acknowledge the great attention which Inspector Reid and the police have given to the case. I leave it to you, the jury, to say, how, when, and by what means the deceased came by her death.'

As if wishing to waste no further time on the matter, the jury brought in the inescapable verdict of 'wilful murder against some person or persons unknown.'

If this was meant to reassure those who had to live and work in the locality, it was a dismal failure. The following day, when local residents read that the police had still got no further in their efforts to identify the savage responsible for cleansing the immediate streets of prostitutes with the aid of a sharp knife, they formed an unruly mob in Berner Street, which took half the available constabulary shift to disperse as they stood braying about the incompetence of the Metropolitan Police in general and 'H' Division in particular. When ordered to move on, the more vociferous of those who had been protesting withdrew to a local pub and formed themselves into the Whitechapel Vigilance Committee, committed to patrolling the dark alleyways by night and dealing in their own way with anyone they found who might be the culprit.

The President of this newly self-appointed Committee, George Lusk, was the one selected to receive, by post in a small cardboard box, what proved to be half a human kidney, the other half of which the sender, who boasted that he came 'from Hell', claimed to have fried and eaten. It was quickly passed on to the authorities and a Dr Openshaw, after conducting comparison tests on the remaining kidney from Catherine Eddowes' corpse, concluded that the two were 'very similar.' Given the information that was already being conveyed to the public by the reporters attending the inquest into the death of Catherine Eddowes, this was not destined to ease the minds of those who were looking carefully all around as they passed from one pool of gaslight to another in the fog-wreathed streets of Whitechapel that Autumn.

This second inquest had commenced on 4th October and was being conducted by the City Coroner, S.F. Langham. The first witness, Catherine's sister, tearfully confirmed the victim's identity and John Kelly told the jury of his seven years living with her in Cooney's Lodging House in Flower and Dean Street and her disappearance on the day prior to her death, ostensibly to visit her daughter in Bermondsey. Later witnesses would tell of her insensible state when found lying drunk in High Street, Aldgate, and her four or so hours in police custody in Bishopsgate Police Station before her release only thirty minutes before the estimated time of her death.

Constable Watkins described how he found the deceased lying on her back in a pool of blood, with 'her clothes thrown up', as he tactfully described it, her throat cut and her stomach ripped open. He was insistent that only fourteen minutes had elapsed since he had last walked past the same spot and seen no body. Inspector Collard then described the subsequent processes of summoning the police surgeon, removing the body to the mortuary, conducting enquiries in the local streets and securing Mitre Square against the prurient eyes of curious spectators. He also made brief reference to the finding, by a Metropolitan Police constable, of the piece of apron in Goulston Street.

The 'star' witness on that first day was police surgeon Dr Frederick Brown, who testified to having called in Dr Phillips from the Met, on account of his familiarity with the previous corpse of Annie Chapman. Death would, Dr Brown testified, have been immediate, as the result of the slashing of the throat. Then it was on to the nauseating details discovered during the post-mortem.

All but a small portion of the victim's uterus had been cut away and it, along with the left kidney, were completely missing by the time that the body had been undressed and prepared for dissection in the mortuary. Despite not being specifically asked, he added that, 'The way the kidney was cut out showed that it was done by somebody who knew what he was about,' although there was no obvious professional use for a spare organ such as a kidney. He opined that the entire process might have taken no more than five minutes and — again somewhat gratuitously — he added, 'I see no reason to doubt that it was the work of one man,' and that the face had been mutilated 'to disfigure the corpse.'

That was the end of the evidence on that first day, but at the resumed inquest a week later, Dr Brown, when invited to do so, expressed the opinion that the atrocities had been inflicted in the place where the body had been found and there could be no question of its having been carried to that spot and dumped.

After several local residents testified to having heard no noise, suspicious or otherwise, from Mitre Square in the early hours of the morning of the discovery of the body, it was the turn of witness Lawende to give his evidence. He testified of having seen the deceased at the Church Passage entrance to Mitre Square shortly after one thirty in the morning, in the company of a man who looked 'rather rough and shabby' and was wearing a peaked cloth cap. He confirmed that he had given a fuller description to the police, but any unsatisfied curiosity that the jury might have experienced regarding the man's identity was rapidly overtaken by the most controversial evidence of all, despite its only marginal evidential value. It was a strong illustration of the desire of the City Police to distance themselves from the mounting criticism of the bumbling ineptitude of their Metropolitan counterparts and it was to do with the portion of once-white and now blood-smeared, apron found in Goulston Street and confirmed as having come from the remaining section of apron still on Catherine Eddowes' body when it was discovered. But it had less to do with the apron portion and more to do with what had been discovered along with it.

Constable Long of the Metropolitan Police and Detective Halse of the City, both advised the jury that the apron portion had been found in the front passageway of a model dwelling house in Goulston Street, where it might well have been thrown by someone passing in the street. But above it, on the wall, someone had written in chalk the phrase: 'The Jews are the men that will not be blamed for nothing.' The conflicting testimonies of the two officers led to controversy over both the spelling and the precise order of the words employed, controversy that could not now be resolved since the writing had been erased on the order of the Metropolitan Police Commissioner Sir Charles Warren.

First of all, while Long was of the opinion that the word had been spelt 'Jews', Halse was adamant that it was spelt 'Juwes', which was allegedly the way that Orthodox Jews might spell it, tending to suggest that its author had been Jewish. Even more in dispute was where precisely in the sentence the word 'not' had occurred. Was it: 'The Jews are the men that will not be blamed for nothing,' implying that they were open to blame for something (and arguably the series of murders for which popular prejudice was already blaming them), or was it: 'The Juwes are not the men that will be blamed for nothing', implying that they were being falsely accused of something they had not done and would be seeking to establish their innocence?

Both officers claimed to have written the sentence down accurately in their notebooks, but the attention of all concerned was diverted by the controversy that surrounded the order given at the time that the offensive sentence be removed before it could become the occasion of a riot.

The fear of this and the responsibility for its removal, were both ascribed to the Metropolitan force, on whose territory Goulston Street was located. When the matter was raised in Parliamentary circles, Sir Charles Warren was obliged to write to his political masters in the Home Office, a month later, justifying his order for the removal of the allegedly racist graffiti on the grounds that 'if that writing had been left, there would have been an onslaught upon the Jews, property would have been wrecked and lives would probably have been lost.'

Perhaps the most blatant piece of blame-shifting that occurred during that inquest arose in connection with the failure to conduct an immediate search of the rooming house in whose front passageway the apron portion had been discovered. A solicitor engaged to represent the 'interests' (which meant, of course, the reputation) of the City of London Police, when asked a question by a jury member regarding why the rest of the dwelling had not been searched immediately upon the discovery of the apron, replied that the City Police had not been advised of the find by their Metropolitan colleagues until two hours afterwards.

In summing up to the jury, and leading them firmly by the nose, the coroner asserted: 'that the crime was a most fiendish one cannot for a moment be doubted, for the miscreant, not satisfied with taking a defenceless woman's life, endeavoured so to mutilate the body as to render it unrecognisable. I presume that you will return a verdict of wilful murder against some person or persons unknown, thereby allowing the police to freely pursue their inquiries and follow up any clue they might obtain. A magnificent reward has been offered and this might be the means of setting people on the track and bringing to speedy justice the creature who committed this atrocious crime.'

He seemed to reflect for a moment, before adding, 'It would be sufficient to return a verdict of wilful murder against some person unknown, inasmuch as the medical evidence conclusively demonstrated that only one person could be implicated.'

The jury duly obliged and one more had been added to the notional misdeeds of the man calling himself 'the Ripper'.

The reference to 'a magnificent reward' was misleading to the point of dishonesty, since, although the City of London had offered five hundred pounds for information leading to an arrest, Sir Charles Warren had argued strenuously for authorisation to offer a much larger one to anyone coming forward with information that would help identify the person responsible for these gruesome atrocities. But he had been refused such authority by Home Secretary Henry Matthews.

As if this disloyalty had not been enough, Sir Charles was also convinced that his authority was being undermined from beneath him, by the man he was most relying on now that his team of detectives was increasingly deployed on the task of identifying and buckling the insane hacker of back-alley prostitutes. James Monro had resigned only a month or two ago from his previous role as Assistant Commissioner, following a lengthy and occasionally vitriolic difference of philosophy between the two men regarding the management, role and independence of the Criminal Investigation Department that had fallen within Monro's remit as Assistant Commissioner. They had also almost come to blows when Warren had blocked the appointment, as an additional Assistant Commissioner, of Monro's close friend Melville McNaghten.

No sooner had Monro's resignation become effective than Home Secretary Matthews had appointed him 'Head of the Detective Service.' This not only allowed Monro to exact his revenge by keeping important information from Warren, but it sent a clear message to the Whitehall police community that in any future confrontation between Warren and Monro, the latter could rely on the support of the Home Secretary, who answered directly to Prime Minister Salisbury, and through him to Queen Victoria herself. Indeed, recent requests from Her Majesty for explanations regarding the failure of London police officers to apprehend the maniac in their midst had all come from the Palace to Salisbury, who had passed them on to Monro while advising the Queen that Warren was the man in ultimate charge of the institutional failure.

Little wonder that the two men sitting in the leather armchairs in Monro's office only days after the Catherine Eddowes inquest felt uncomfortable. Not only did they have to explain why they had so far failed to lock up the Ripper, but they were aware that anything they said that might possibly be used to undermine their ultimate superior officer would be put to good effect by their own immediate boss.

'I fail to see how the lunatic has so far managed to evade capture,' Monro complained as he glared pointedly at Abberline.

'That question were better directed at Reid,' Abberline growled.

'Who would be better placed to answer it,' Reid retorted, 'if you weren't undermining me at every move.'

'That's enough — both of you!' Monro instructed them. 'If the pair of you can't work in harmony, at the very top of this investigation, that sentiment will clearly leak down through the ranks and they'll all begin taking sides. It's bad enough that we have to work with the City because your resident madman took his penchant for sharp knives to the wrong side of Aldgate. Reid, how many men have you got deployed on the streets?'

'All of them,' Reid complained, 'to the point at which normal policing is at a standstill. The pickpockets, totties, burglars and footpads can operate with impunity while my men lurk under lampposts trying to look as if they're about to apprehend the culprit. That seems to be keeping the lid on the local Yid-haters and vigilantes, but unless the person responsible cares to step out under a gaslight and wave his knife in full view of a uniformed constable, we don't have a realistic hope in Hell of catching him in the act.'

'There's no doubt we're dealing with the same man for every one of these outrages?' Monro enquired.

'So it would seem,' Reid replied before Abberline could offer the same opinion, 'although there's a curious difference in methodology between them. The one we believe to have been the first victim — Martha Tabram — was simply killed by a single stab to the heart, although the assailant played "needlepoint" with a penknife as an encore. Next came Polly Nichols, who had her throat cut and was subjected to minor surgery in what was almost broad daylight before we believe that the attacker was disturbed. With Annie Chapman he had more time and various organs were removed and retained after he cut her throat. Then came what the press dubbed 'the double event'; Elizabeth Stride, who also had her throat cut before the killer was again disturbed, followed by the latest in the series, Catherine Eddowes — another longer piece of anatomising and the removal of, among other things, the kidney which was sent to a local vigilante group.'

'Anything to add?' Monro asked Abberline, who shrugged.

'Yes and no. We're not sure that the Stride and Eddowes killings were by the same man, or even if they occurred in the order that everyone's assuming.'

'In the rumoured belief that this person has medical knowledge, have you tried all the local hospitals for loony doctors?'

'Disturbingly, we identified five, all still let loose on patients, but all with immaculate alibis,' Reid replied.

'Sailors?'

Abberline guffawed, before apologising and explaining the reason for his mirth. 'Do you know how many docks there are within hacking distance of Whitechapel and how many vessels come and go during the course of a week, sir?'

'Point taken, but keep trying. I'd hate to have to advise the noisier elements of the East End that it's probably one of their own.'

'The ease with which the offender evades detection certainly suggests a detailed knowledge of the area and particularly where the back alleys lead to and from,' Reid confirmed.

'All the victims have been prostitutes, that right?'

'Correct so far,' Reid confirmed, 'but of course they're the easiest targets. They make themselves available in doorways and pubs to any passing male and they take them up dark alleys to earn their few wretched pennies. My biggest fear is that he'll branch out and start attacking more law-abiding folk on their way to and from legitimate activities. At least our Ripper is keeping the numbers down in the pubs and the doss houses are full after eleven in the evening.'

'Anything else you think I should know?' Monro enquired.

When both men sadly shook their heads, the meeting was brought to a close.

'Keep going, both of you, preferably both in the same direction at the same time. Bring me the head of Jack the Ripper.'

Chapter Eighteen

Esther carried the bowl of water carefully up the staircase and into her room, placing it on the washstand, then leaning forward and splashing her eyes in an attempt to remove the redness. It was all very well crying for three days, if the cause was right, but the evidence would have to be removed before she could venture up to Rosen's with her latest batch of finished work. If it came to that, she would need to clear her vision sufficiently to complete the last commission, a frock coat into which an extra inside pocket had been inserted and which needed to be hand-stitched to a proper finish.

She raised her head and looked out of the narrow window down into the yard, where it was drizzling. There was mud on the ground, left by a wagon that had recently unloaded more carcasses that would eventually feed a hundred cats for a month and her mind flew back to the mud that always seemed to lie on Church Lane. She would have to stop brooding on what might have been, she ordered herself sternly. Her brain received the message, but her heart was reluctant to leave Barking.

Her mind began to replay that final drama yet again, as if she hadn't spent the past three days going over and over it, like some awful book that was terrifying to read, but which she couldn't bring herself to put down. The ominous silence of that ride home, Jack trying everything in his power to get her to speak; her fear of doing so in case she said awful things that put their relationship beyond retrieval. Perhaps she would have been better off saying them and breaking that final thread, rather than living on in a hopeless dream of something magical happening — perhaps waking up to find that it had all been a horrid nightmare, or a visit from Constance Enright to apologise for what she had said and thought.

No chance, she reminded herself. For one thing, Jack's mother wouldn't be seen dead in a hovel like this. More to the point, she had been perfectly right to seek to protect her son from an unwise match with a Jewess who lived in a common lodging house and took in sewing for a living. For all the good looks that others insisted on telling her that she possessed, she was still a *pischerke* — a nobody. One day her looks would fade and she would still be a seamstress at heart, an orphan relying on others for her survival. Jack might amuse himself by playing at being a policeman, but he was from a different world from hers and one day he would wake up to himself and take his rightful place in society. Then how would he feel, making his way in polite social circles with a wife whose origins had to be tactfully hidden from their suspicious friends?

Not that Jack had even mentioned marriage, so why was she fooling herself? His mother might think that he was about to propose to Esther, but that was probably just a mother's ambitious wish for her son to be settled in life, with grandchildren to dote on her as she passed into old age. Now, of course, there could be no question of anything like that. Still, she had learned one thing; never be too open-hearted or generous with one's affections. Jack had seemed too good to be true and as it turned out he was. *Head down*, she told herself, *get on with that sewing and then get up to Rosen's for your money — that's your real place in life.*

She hadn't heard the first gentle tapping on her door and only became aware of it as it became louder and more insistent, accompanied by the strident voice of Sadie Thompson. 'Get off yer arse, lady — yer copper's 'ere ter see yer!'

Her heart leapt into her mouth and she hastily brushed down her dress and looked into the hand mirror on her small dressing table to see if the redness still showed. Then she stopped herself in her tracks. If Jack Enright thought he could come crawling round here, seeking to persuade her that he really did love her for herself, when in fact he was only following Mama's instructions to get himself a pretty wife to hang off his arm, then he could damn well look somewhere else.

She threw open the door and confronted Sadie. 'Tell him I don't want to see him and to take his uniformed presence somewhere else, where the neighbours won't think the worst.'

'It's not the one wi' the uniform,' Sadie advised her. 'It's the older one what were wearin' 'is own clothes the last time 'e were 'ere.'

'Percy?'

'I don't know 'is bloody name, do I? Best get down inter the kitchen.'

With some reluctance, but driven by curiosity, Esther smartened herself up and went downstairs. Percy Enright sat at the table and looked up nervously as Esther breezed in, trying her best to look unconcerned. Percy smiled weakly as he looked into her eyes.

'Looks like you've been crying,' he observed.

'None of your business,' Esther advised him curtly, 'and if you're here to tell me how sorry Jack is for what his mother said and for leading me up the garden path, don't waste your breath. This pretty little seamstress can talk for herself, but has no message for your nephew that's fit for a lady to utter, or a gentleman like yourself to hear.'

Percy's face hardened slightly. 'You can be ruthless when you want to be, can't you? What exactly did Constance say to you that's caused such a rift between you and Jack?'

'You heard what I said in the garden last Sunday. She obviously thinks of me as a slum girl setting her hat at a wealthy boy. She must have got that idea from Jack and I obviously couldn't pursue our relationship in those circumstances, always wondering what he really thinks of me. Did he send you up here to see how I'm dealing with the truth?'

Percy shook his head sadly. 'I haven't seen him since Sunday. Nobody has. He's shut himself in his room at his lodgings, refusing all food. His only communication was a note to Edmund Reid asking for permission to take his annual leave all in one instalment, effective immediately. That expires next Monday and if he doesn't report for duty by then, he'll be thrown off the force. So stop feeling so sorry for yourself and grow up!'

'Are you here just to tell me that?' she challenged him. 'If so, please be aware that I've grown up more since Sunday than I ever thought possible and now I can get on with my life knowing what my true value is to others.'

'And your value to the community?' he enquired enigmatically.

'Meaning?'

'Meaning I need to find Mary Kelly.'

'You were the one who told me about her — surely you know where she can be found?'

'Yes and no,' Percy replied. 'Somewhere along Dorset Street, which is the biggest rabbit warren in Spitalfields, the last time I looked. But she's our only link to what Pearly Poll and her slasher are really up to.'

'I thought you'd given up with her,' Esther reminded him. 'According to what I hear from what other people read in the papers, even Inspector Reid thinks your killer of prostitutes is a random lunatic.'

'Maybe he does,' Percy explained, 'but he still wants to do Poll for procuring abortions and a win like that might cheer him up. He's making life pretty miserable for the rest of us, gromphing around the station and yelling back at us whenever we say anything intended to cheer him up. A bit like the way you're behaving at the moment, actually.'

'So why can't you go into Dorset Street with the full might of the law, kick down a few doors and batter people over the head till they give you the truth?'

'If that's the image that Jack gave you of how we police work, then I'm very sad,' Percy replied with a shake of the head. 'We're a bit more subtle when dealing with law-abiding people than we are when we're breaking up street brawls.'

'So why can't you just go up there and ask some important questions?' she demanded, forcing an ironic laugh from Percy.

'This is Spitalfields, young lady. Do you know what happens when a police officer enters an area like Dorset Street and starts asking questions?'

'Obviously not.'

'Well, let me tell you. It's like sneezing into a box of chicken feathers. They scatter in all directions, give themselves false names, deny even their own grandmothers and run like Hell as soon as our backs are turned.'

'So why do you need my assistance?'

'I was very impressed with your performance that day in the pub, when we came across Pearly Poll. You know how to blend in with these people and ...'

'Because I'm one of them myself?' Esther interrupted him with a bitter grimace.

'Do you want to hear what I'm proposing, or are you going to wallow in your own self-pity the whole day? If so, I'll take my leave now.'

'Sorry, carry on.'

'As I was saying, no-one's going to suspect an ordinary young lady like yourself — although, let me add that I think you're far from ordinary — anyway, an ordinary young lady like yourself seeking out someone who knows someone else who can organise an abortion. If we can confirm that the person whose name Mary Kelly was given really was Pearly Poll, then we have lawful justification for kicking her door down.'

Esther slid into the spare chair and decided to come clean. 'I've already got beyond that point on my own initiative. After you left me in the White Hart, I pretended to Pearly Poll that you were my fancy man, that you'd got me in the family way and that you were prepared to give me a tenner for an abortion. I was supposed to meet her back at the White Hart last night to take it to the next stage, but with everything that happened on Sunday I didn't have the heart and quite frankly I couldn't see the point any more.'

Percy's eyes had opened wide at this revelation. 'Have you any idea how much danger you were courting, confronting the woman like that? She may well be controlling our Ripper, who almost certainly killed your friend Martha and women like Poll can normally rustle up an army of thugs to silence anyone who gets in the way of their illegal activities.'

'I don't think she suspects me,' Esther countered, 'but even if she does, the fact that I've already got her to more or less admit that she does abortions means that you don't need Mary Kelly any more, doesn't it?'

'Don't take this the wrong way,' Percy requested, 'but it would only be your word against Poll's. We need to find some women she's already performed the service for and perhaps get confirmation that it was done in that room in George Yard Buildings and the key to getting all that may be Mary Kelly. That's my hope anyway. What I need you to do is to find her for me.'

'If I do, will you do something for me?'

'That will obviously depend,' he replied cautiously.

'Nothing unlawful, although perhaps something beyond even your capabilities. I've written Jack a short note — could you see that he gets it?'

'I could push it under his door, certainly. That's as far as I've managed to get so far in my attempts to talk some sense into him.'

Esther ran quickly upstairs and grabbed the note she had written five times before being satisfied that she could not improve upon it in any way. A collection of pens, paper and ink were her one luxury in life and for once she was putting them to better use than the idle scribbling of poems that occasionally came into her head in quiet moments gazing down into a cats' meat factory yard.

Two hours later Jack was intrigued to hear his uncle hammering yet again on his door, yelling, 'If this doesn't pull you to your senses, I'll be down in the tea shop next to the bakery for the next half hour', and watched a thin envelope sliding under his door. He noted the neat handwriting of his name on the envelope and the perfume in which it was doused brought back heavenly memories, so he tore it open.

The tears he was ashamed to shed began again as he read what Esther had written.

Dear Jack,

Please excuse this somewhat cowardly way of telling you what I was unable to do to your face. First be assured that I love you with all my heart and all my being. But I now realise, with deep sadness and longing, that we cannot have a future together.

We are simply from different worlds. Yours is a world of wealth and security, whereas I am penniless, existing from day to day in a rented room overlooking a miserable yard in a backstreet slum, scraping together a living from sewing other peoples' clothes. If we were to remain together and perhaps even become husband and wife, how could you explain my background to your comfortably-off friends in the society to which you belong, but I do not?

I don't like to think for one moment that you were only interested in me for my body or my looks and I will not insult you by suggesting that you were, but apart from those, what could I bring into a relationship and perhaps even a marriage? One day my looks will fade and what would be left? If love for you could be a suitable substitute, then I have that in such abundance that I have to keep stopping for the tears even while I'm writing this. But, simple seamstress that I am, even I know that in this harsh world that we both inhabit, my devotion to you could never make up for my lack of breeding.

Please accept my word that I never looked upon you as a step up in life, or an easy way out of the backstreets of Spitalfields. I could have lived as your wife in the meanest lodging house in East London and been the happiest woman in the world. But I cannot ask that of you and I could not spend the rest of my days wondering if you looked upon me simply as an adventuress who got lucky.

So goodbye, my darling Jack. Please give your mother my sincere apologies for my rudeness and know that I will always care for you.

Esther

While Jack was splashing tears all over her letter as he held it to his face and breathed in the lingering perfume, Esther was striding, head down, up Brick Lane, avoiding wagons and fellow pedestrians in her determination to reach the Rosen's premises in Lamb Street with her latest completed commissions before the clouds that were still delivering drizzle with a depressing determination decided to hurl down something more substantial. She reached the building slightly out of breath and paused for a moment to slow the pace of her heartbeat. She looked up at the familiar three stories that had once been home and noted that Isaac and Ruth had finally got all the windows installed, although unless they spent a fortune on scrubbing, the stonework would forever retain the scorch marks from that dreadful night.

She pushed open the front door and walked in, calling out as she did so, '*Shalom*, Isaac, it's only me — Esther.'

Isaac or Ruth would normally come through from the back into the large ground-floor room that had once housed half a dozen sewing machines, each with a seamstress working away busily at the treadles. Today the room was empty as usual, but from behind the curtains that now divided the original room could be heard muttered Yiddish curses in a man's voice.

She shouted even louder and Isaac's head appeared between the gap, complete with his customary kippah.

'Good day, *tochter*. And how does this day find you? Your face it is sad, yet you smile. Why is this?'

'It doesn't matter. Here's my latest completed work — do you have more for me?'

'Who can tell, in that *patschkerai* of paper that is behind the curtain? Oy vey, if God had intended me to be a keeper of books, he would not have given me the fingers of a tailor.'

'Doesn't Ruth still do your paperwork?'

'In good times she does. But today, as for the past week or so, Ruth she is, how should I say, not so good that she can rise from her bed. Will you go up and visit her? You were always like a real *tochter* to the both of us, since God did not choose to bless us with any of our own.'

'Of course I will, Isaac. Then I'll help you with that paperwork.'

She climbed the narrow stairway to the bedroom on the first floor that had always belonged to Isaac and Ruth and had been one of the few rooms to survive serious damage in the fire. Ruth lay half sleeping, half whimpering, in her bed, but seemed to stop when she heard the footfall on the wooden boards in the doorway. She turned her head and seemed relieved to discover that it was only Esther as she held out a bony hand covered in age spots.

'Ah, *bubbeleh*, so good you should come and see me.'

'Are you in pain?' Esther asked with concern. 'As I came up the stairs, I heard you crying out.'

'Thank the good Lord it was not Isaac. He must not know, since he is such a good man and he tries so hard for my happiness.'

'Mustn't know what, Aunt Ruth?'

'I am dying, child. I need no doctor to tell me that soon I will be no more. Then what will Isaac do?'

'I'll look after him, *mume*, I promise you.'

'Such a good child. You will not tell him about the pain?'

'Of course not, but surely ... '

'He has many worries already, but he is a good man.'

'He seems to be having trouble with the accounts down there.'

Ruth chuckled, then screwed her face with the pain of shaking her sparse bony frame. 'Isaac was never the one for the figures — except mine, when I was his *kale*. I thought he would give me many *kinder*, but it was not to be. Then you came into our lives and you must help him, since he is your *foter* now.'

'I promise I will,' Esther assured her, 'and now is there something I can get for you?'

'A glass of water, perhaps. And peace of mind for Isaac.'

Back downstairs, hoping not to inadvertently disclose just how sick Ruth was and how permanent the arrangement was likely to become, Esther offered to come up to the business every day and look after the books until Ruth was well again. The old man was almost in tears as he took her two hands in his and kissed them.

'Such a *mentsh*, always. Can you start today?'

'Once I've run one more errand, *foter* Isaac. I'll be back within the hour, I promise.'

Her mind reeling with the implications of what she had just learned about Ruth and the responsibility she had taken on, but glad that she had plenty to take her mind off Jack, Esther walked a little further along Lamb Street, then made the left turn down Crispin Street until the entrance to Dorset Street came into view. Taking a deep breath, she walked up to two teenage girls who were doing a fair impression of holding up the wall at an entrance into a courtyard while exchanging a pipe whose contents they were taking it in turns to inhale. They eyed her with dumb curiosity as she walked up to them with the best cheery smile she could manage and enquired after Mary Kelly.

'She normally only does men,' the one with very few remaining teeth replied with a knowing smirk.

'I'm not seeking a hairdresser,' Esther replied starchily. 'I need to ask her something important.'

'What's it worth?' the other girl demanded.

'Forget it,' Esther replied as she turned and walked smartly away. She had only gone a few yards when one of them shouted after her departing back.

'If yer means the fat whore, try Miller's Court.'

Miller's Court came into view towards the centre of the street and it appeared to be somewhat above the normal run of lodging houses, in the sense that the downstairs rooms were marginally more spacious and had windows that opened. Through one of them could be heard the tuneless attempts of some woman or other to render some sort of folk song that sounded vaguely obscene, so far as Esther could deduce from the slurred words. She walked into the passageway that led to the rooms and just as her eyes were focussing in the gloom she narrowly avoided tripping over a youth propped up against the wall, cutting a length of leather into a sole for his boot, employing a sharp knife. Esther looked at the blade and shuddered as she recalled what had happened to Martha and the other women in recent months; then she realised that the youth was staring in fascination at her bosom and took advantage of having his full attention.

'I'm looking for Mary Kelly.'

'Mary the Irish whore?' the youth enquired.

'That's the one,' Esther replied, since the description sounded appropriate.

'That's 'er singin' in there,' the youth responded with a nod towards a ground floor rear room that bore the number 13. 'She earns more openin' 'er legs than she ever will openin' 'er fuckin' mouth,' he added by way of musical critique.

'I paid a penny for that lump of horsemeat in a crust, so eat the bloody thing,' Percy instructed Jack. 'And that's an order from a superior officer.'

'I'm not in the mood for eating a pie,' Jack complained, 'or anything else, for that matter.'

'You're as bad as that young lady of yours,' Percy grumbled. 'I feel like putting the two of you next to each other and banging your heads together.'

'It would be worth it, just to be standing next to her again,' Jack replied, his eyes fixed on the passing traffic as they sat in the tea shop at the corner of Mansell Street and Aldgate.

'She seemed pretty devastated herself,' Percy observed. 'I'm sure it wouldn't take much more than a smart rap on the noggin to bring her round. It's as if somebody put poison in her head and it'll take a while to work its way out.'

'I gather you've seen her recently,' Jack replied morosely, 'which is more than I have.'

'Of course I have,' Percy confirmed. 'How do you think you came to get that letter? What did she have to say, if I might enquire?'

'Only that we're finished,' Jack mumbled into the remains of his tea.

'Did she say why, exactly?'

'Only some rubbish about not being good enough for me and that I might not be looking beyond her beauty at the real person underneath.'

'And are you?'

'Of course I am,' Jack assured him. 'I could have had lots of girls in the past, but none of them ever appealed to me. There's something about Esther that holds you captive and won't let you go. Not just her obvious beauty — something from deep inside, like she was made specially by God, just for me.'

'I know what you mean,' Percy advised him with a smile. 'Believe it or not, your Aunt Beattie was once such a girl. The minute I laid eyes on her I was hooked and when she first began talking to me, I was hauled in and landed. She and Esther have the same charm that's fatal to any man with half a brain.'

'What would you call it, uncle?'

'Lively intelligence, that's what.'

'Yeah, that sort of says it exactly,' Jack agreed. 'But how can I get her to realise that I love her, not just her looks?'

'You could start by taking an interest in the latest job she's doing for us.'

Jack's jaw dropped. 'What do you mean?'

'She's agreed to find Mary Kelly for me, then we might get enough evidence to put the buckles on Pearly Poll.'

'Did you allocate any men to trail her and make sure she doesn't come to any harm?'

'No — why should I?'

'Because I love her, that's why — and you could have just put her in grave danger.'

Chapter Nineteen

Esther made the brisk journey to and from the Rosens' premises many times in the days that followed. The accounts were no great challenge to her, particularly since a significant proportion of the mending work that constituted the bulk of the business was destined for her anyway, while Isaac sat at one of the surviving sewing machines making suits to order and humming folk tunes from his youth as he worked away, blissfully unaware that his life partner was fading away one floor above him.

Esther made sure to visit Aunt Ruth at least twice a day, to bring her comfort and to attempt to get her to eat. Some days she was successful, but most days not and she eventually managed to persuade a reluctant Isaac that perhaps a physician should be called in. On his first visit, after a whispered plea from Ruth, he ordered Isaac from the sick room while he made his examination, then advised Esther, who had been allowed to remain, that she would need to purchase morphia pills from the local pharmacy, along with substantial quantities of laudanum for the times between the four-hourly swallowing of pills when the pain got too bad. He also took Esther to one side and advised her that the old lady had only a few weeks left.

Although her mind was kept fully occupied during the working day, keeping Isaac's books of accounts, making discreet trips to the local pharmacy and handling any clothing alterations and repairs that came their way while Isaac continued his tailoring, Esther tried unsuccessfully to convince herself that her mind was playing tricks on her as she walked for twenty minutes or so each day between her work and her lodgings, as she had the uncanny feeling that someone was following her. Her vital importance to the kindly old couple who were effectively her adoptive parents was such that she could not for one moment contemplate not making the trip every working day and it was of limited consolation that Isaac insisted on paying her a weekly wage four times what she had been earning as a casual out-worker. But she dreaded the trips there and back and more than once considered asking whether she could move into her old room on the second floor, which had never been renovated. It had taken much of the ferocity of the fire some eighteen months previously and would take a great deal of work and expense to make liveable again.

It had begun with a woman who had clearly been following her on the day when she'd located Mary Kelly and then lost no time in passing on the address by means of a note left for Percy Enright at Leman Street police station. Apart from the courage she was required to summon up in order to re-enter the place that contained lingering memories of happier days, she was fearful that she might accidentally encounter Jack and was unsure how her heart and mouth would behave if she came face to face with him again.

Then on the way back up Commercial Street she became aware of a rough-looking labourer who darted into the nearest alleyway every time she stopped and looked behind her — a man who still seemed to be following her intently as she turned into George Street and all but ran for the safety of the common entrance to number 19.

Every day there seemed to be someone close behind her until she turned and the shadowy figure would seem to melt into a shop doorway, or change direction. She never got a good look at whoever it was and she could not be sure that it was the same person on each occasion, but it was almost always a man and she needed no further incentive to keep closely to her room with the door locked once she got home for the day, by which time she was usually so exhausted that she simply fell into bed and passed out until the sun woke her up at daybreak the following day.

She had been trying hard to keep her mind off Jack as the weeks passed, but her stomach lurched with excitement when news of him was passed on to her by Percy Enright during a surprise visit one Saturday. He had sent word up from the kitchen that he need to speak to her and she had taken a deep breath before descending the single flight of stairs.

'How are you, Esther?'

'Very well, thank you. It was as well that you called when you did, because I'm now employed fulltime by the people who used to commission sewing work from me on a casual basis and I'm seriously thinking of moving into living accommodation above the work premises themselves. But today is the Jewish Sabbath, so I'm not at work, as you can see.'

Percy's face became more gloomy as he advised her that she was not the only one who seemed destined to move. 'I'm afraid Jack resigned from the police force once his leave expired and we haven't seen him since,' he advised her. 'His mother's going frantic because he hasn't shown up in Barking yet and that was over three weeks ago. But he must have found work somewhere else, because his landlady finally admitted that he hadn't yet moved out of his room in Mansell Street, so I'm thinking of laying in wait for him one day and following him to his new place of employment. That's the least I can do for his mother, irresponsible idiot that he is.'

'Talking of people being followed,' Esther butted in, 'I think that someone's following me every day as I walk up and back from Lamb Street. I can't be certain, but neither can I shake off the suspicion.'

'Do you want me to organise for someone to look out for your safety?' Percy enquired.

Esther shook her head. 'Thanks, but that won't be necessary. No-one's going to attack me in the street in broad daylight. It was only really obvious that I was being followed that day I found Mary Kelly's address for you. Did you manage to get what you needed from her?'

Percy shook his head. 'She clammed up completely, refused to say a word, denied seeking an abortion from anyone and insisted that we leave. I tried again a few days later, on my own this time and she slammed the door in my face.'

'So you're no nearer to charging Poll with abortions? How are you going with those awful stabbings?'

'There haven't been any more, thank God, so hopefully whoever it was considers their work to be finished.'

'Well, good luck anyway. Would you like a cup of tea?'

'No, thank you all the same. Any message for Jack if I manage to find him?'

'Tell him that I'm now making my way in the garment industry, that I still love him and always will and that I can recommend a good tailor in Lamb Street,' she smiled bravely.

Chapter Twenty

Mary Kelly was stony broke again and it was almost certainly due to her generous nature. Joe Barnett had left her in the lurch, walking out over a week ago after Mary let yet another of her prostitute friends spend the night in their room because she didn't have the fourpence for a doss in a common lodging house. Mary hadn't eaten any food worthy of that name for two days, although she'd had more than her fair share of gin down the road in the Ten Bells earlier that evening. She was supposed to be saving enough money to take the boat back to her native Ireland, but as fast as she got it she would spend it on the grog that dulled her senses against the thing she hated most, which was laying down for men. But like most women in her position it was all she had to trade with and she could usually command a slightly higher price, despite her rapidly fading former beauty, because she had a room of her own in which her mark could enjoy her lying down naked, rather than with her skirts hitched up in some smelly back alley with the ever-present risk of being disturbed.

If she could only raise a few pounds she could break the vicious circle. With a few pounds in her purse she could go home to her family in Limerick and wouldn't need to rent herself out to every drunken sailor or fat businessman who had sixpence to spare. If she wasn't on the game she wouldn't need to drink and she could keep most of the money she scraped together from charring in the houses of the more well to do 'up west', or lining up in the casual queue for a day's steaming sweaty labour in the local laundry. Then she could take the passage home.

Right now, she needed sixpence if she was to put some coal in the tiny fireplace that came with her room. It was after two in the morning and there were less people in Commercial Street than there had been earlier, so her chances of picking up a decent mark were considerably reduced. But as she walked past the open door of the Queen's Head a smartly dressed man lurched out and the two of them stood eyeing each other briefly before Mary took the initiative.

'Looking for a short time, lovey?'

The man nodded and Mary figured out that he was probably good for sixpence. Some sort of Jewish commercial traveller, Mary calculated with experienced eyes. Probably a long way from his home in the Midlands, probably randy with alcohol and probably hadn't had a woman — least of all his wife — for weeks. Too easy for a woman who might still seem attractive after a night of drinking.

'I've got a place round the corner, but it'll cost yer sixpence,' she announced. No point in messing about in polite chat at this time in the morning. The man nodded again and moved forward to put his arm over her shoulder as she led the way. He was carrying a small parcel in his other hand and seemed reluctant to talk as she led him into Dorset Street and on down to Millers Court. They stopped once under a lamp post and Mary leaned forward and kissed him lightly on the lips; his response was to grope at her breast over her cheap blouse and she reached down towards his groin. He wasn't hard yet, but Mary would soon remedy that.

They entered the room and Mary locked the door, smiling as he stood there expectantly.

'Do you mind if I light the fire, lovey?' she enquired. 'Then I can take all me clothes off and make it nicer for you.'

She would need to use up the last of her wood, but she could get coals in the morning and the room was damp and chilly in the early November night. She lit the fire and once it was blazing nicely she swiftly peeled off her outer garments in order to engage his full interest, before reminding him, as lightly as she knew how, that, 'That'll be sixpence, lovey.'

Her smile froze as she turned and saw the long knife appear from inside the parcel and the eyes of her mark open wide with excitement as he stepped forward.

Chapter Twenty-One

The funeral service was over and Esther had no tears left to cry as she gently took Isaac's arm and led him back out to the coach that had conveyed Ruth Rosen's body to the Jews' Cemetery in Brady Street. He was moaning gently in his own tongue and Esther could only understand part of it as the horse plodded its way into Bucks Court and she tried to recall which of the Ripper's victims had been found lying here all those weeks ago. A Ripper who appeared to have tired of his gruesome activities; so hopefully life in Whitechapel and Spitalfields could return to normal and Esther could begin to make plans to move into the premises in Lamb Street to look after the weeping wreck of a man who had been so kind to her when she most needed him and who now needed her.

They were halfway down Hanbury Street when she heard the newsvendor's faint call. She hoped she had misheard what he was yelling at the top of his voice, all but drowned as it was by the combined din of carriages and wagons. She wound down the window sash and leaned out as the coach trundled past the news stand at the junction with Brick Lane. There was only one headline on the board by his side and it left no-one in doubt as to the breaking sensation that was filling the evening editions.

'Ripper Strikes Again! Horrible Outrage in Spitalfields!'

She called for the coach driver to halt, leapt from the carriage, extracted a penny shakily from her purse and returned to Isaac's side as she began to read. He was still moaning and crying, cocooned in his own misery, so she had time to read as the coach swayed and clattered the last few yards across

Commercial Street, where Hanbury Street became Lamb Street. She had enough time to learn the name of the victim and the address of the latest atrocity and she prayed to God for forgiveness for having been the one who had made it possible.

Fred Abberline was in a mood best described as 'cold fury' as he confronted Percy Enright and Edmund Reid in the latter's office.

'We have to buckle this maniac without delay, before we all lose our jobs! Parliament's calling for Warren's head and they'll probably get it. My guess is that Monro will get the top job, then God help all of us if he brings McNaghten in to head up the CID. He may have been good at bullying punka wallahs on Indian tea plantations, but he knows bugger all about police work. I give it five minutes before he's telling us how to do our jobs and demanding our resignations if we can't catch a simple slasher of prostitutes.'

'Are we sure it's the same man?' Reid enquired, more in hope than expectation.

Abberline snorted. 'Either him or his apprentice, although this one was undoubtedly the worst. In my years on the force I've seen some gruesome sights, as no doubt you both have, but believe me when I say that this was the most disgusting destruction of a fellow human that I've ever encountered. Her guts were all over the room and the place smelt like an abattoir.'

'We've already flooded the streets with uniforms,' Reid reminded him. 'Short of giving every street tottie a personal bodyguard, I'm not sure what we can do next.'

'Somebody must know something,' Enright pointed out unnecessarily. 'If only Warren had been allowed to offer that reward, we might have got a vital lead. Can we not organise some sort of indemnity for anyone coming forward with information?'

'What you'll get then,' Abberline reminded him, 'is a long queue of jokers trying to peach on their neighbours in the vain hope that we officially forgive them their sins before we can test the information they supply.'

'Do you have any better suggestion?' Enright challenged him.

Abberline shook his head. 'All we have is the information we got from witnesses around Dorset Street last night. The victim was last seen with the same man described in connection with some of the other killings — five foot six or seven, "shabby genteel" in appearance, possible Jewish or at least "foreign looking", with a moustache which varies in colour from ginger to black, according to the light it was seen in.'

'He must have been covered from head to toe in blood from what you tell us of the state of the victim,' Enright observed.

It was Reid's turn to snort. 'According to various medical experts who've testified at the inquests so far that may not be the case if the killer attacked from behind and leaned backwards when the jugular started spurting.'

'This one may have been different,' Enright persisted. 'This was the first — and please God the last — to be committed indoors. You can't sneak up behind your victim when you're in the same room as them.'

'According to the police surgeon — Phillips, again — Mary Kelly died some time between three and four in the morning,' Abberline advised them. 'Assuming that the killer didn't wait around for the morning paper, he'd be long out of there before daybreak, with only the usual early workers on their way through the streets. Nobody reports having seen anyone unusual at around that time, although, just to make our lives more difficult, one of her neighbours swore she saw the victim herself walking down Dorset Street towards Commercial Street at around four thirty. She didn't get to speak with her because she — the witness, that is — was on her way to get her husband's breakfast.'

'So we have no way of moving this forward?' Red enquired. 'Is there nothing we can do?'

'You any good at praying?' Allerdine enquired sarcastically.

Jack Enright slid further into the alleyway across the road from where Esther was supervising the loading of her few possessions onto the carrier's cart and made an intelligent guess that Esther was changing her address for that building in Lamb Street where she seemed to spend every day. So much for happy memories, he reminded himself, as he recalled playing cards with Esther in the small kitchen at number 19 and calling around for her on Sunday afternoons, his heart full of hope and ambition that somehow his mouth had never got around to expressing in words. If only he'd managed to pop the question before his interfering mother had opened her own stupid mouth; if only he'd made it clear to Esther that he was entranced by her personality, her courage in the face of the adversities that life had thrown at her, her positive attitude towards life in general. But then, life was full of 'if onlys', like his now defunct police career.

So what was he doing here, out of work and aimlessly following Esther like some love-lorn puppy? His only answer to that question was that what was left of his world would come apart completely if he didn't get to see her every day and reassure himself that she was still alive. But what would he do if he saw her one day with another young man? No, he couldn't allow himself to even think that dreadful thought and as long as she was locked away in that burned out old ruin of a former tailor's shop whose name — 'Rosen's Bespoke' — could still be made out in the charred stonework above the door, then she'd not have any opportunity to meet someone else and Jack would be secure in the only world left to him — watching her daily from what he hoped was a discreet distance.

The carrier handed down the last of Esther's bundles and she extracted the three shillings from her purse and thanked him for his assistance. Then she walked sadly into the place that was to be her new home. 'Sadly' because she'd been obliged to say goodbye to the happy memories of Jack's Sunday visits and her inspired nights spent writing poetry about how much she loved him. She wasn't to know then that she wasn't the right 'sort' for him and that 'happy ever afters' weren't intended for the poor — at least, not the honest ones.

Isaac smiled as he came from behind the curtain and saw her carrying in the final bundle.

'You may have the room above us, *tochter*. For me it is full of memories that are not now the happiest, but for you — who knows?'

'And where will you sleep?' she enquired suspiciously.

'For an old *zokn* like myself, sleep is not something that is much required. Your old room can be made fit to house my old frame when I need rest and now that the business is back on its feet, thanks to you, we can perhaps call in the painter. Or perhaps I still have skill with a paintbrush. Do you know that when we first moved into here, I was the one who made good with the brush?'

'I do, because you told me,' Esther replied with a smile. *More than once*, she added silently.

At least Isaac had been correct regarding the state of the business. Once Esther made it possible for accounts to be paid before garments were actually handed over, their incomings began exceeding their outgoings by encouragingly increasing amounts, as Esther's weekly account balances accurately confirmed. Isaac insisted on sharing the success with her and Esther could never before in her life have even dreamed of being in receipt of five pounds per week, a sum she stored carefully in a tin box under her bed, as some sort of consolation for still being a spinster seamstress, albeit a highly paid one.

Isaac was also still a good cook, if somewhat *kosher* in tastes, and Esther's once slim frame began to fill out as she gratefully accepted *matzoh* ball soup one day and cheese and potato *boreka* the next. It was as well that she was able to let out her gowns and jackets from time to time. Jack would hardly recognise her now, she mused, before reminding herself that he probably already had another young lady on his arm — one more acceptable to a certain party in Barking.

In the third month of her new life Esther was on the far side of the curtain working on her accounts when she heard the front door open and Isaac speaking in his quiet gentle way with a loud-mouthed woman who was demanding something that Esther could not quite hear above the noise of the street traffic audible through the still open door. Then Isaac's puzzled face appeared through the gap.

'This lady, she is asking for you, *bubbeleh*. If she is offering you work, please do not forget the needs of your old *foter*.'

Puzzled, Esther stepped out from behind the curtain and found herself face to face with Pearly Poll.

Chapter Twenty-Two

'What do you want?' Esther demanded, her heart in her mouth.

'Fer all yer boss knows, I'm 'ere to enquire after the price fer a dress ter be altered,' Poll smiled back as she all but whispered, 'so let's pretend that I am and step out inter the street for a minute or two.'

Assuring Isaac that she would be back in less than a minute, Esther accompanied Poll outside, where, amid the noise of the mid-morning traffic trundling and rattling up and down Lamb Street, Poll looked Esther all over before commenting, 'Yer look as if yer 'ad that little service performed that you was askin' me about durin' our last little conversation, so who did it?'

Esther thought quickly, giving thanks to God for her foresight in looking the point up in an old medical book she found lying around at the Rosens' house, mainly out of curiosity, but just in case.

'I was fortunate enough to lose it naturally,' she advised Poll. 'At least, I hope so. There was this horrible rush of blood and something worse I think and then I started bleeding as normal last month, so I hope I'm in the clear. Do you think I am?'

'Who knows,' Poll observed as she continued to stare at Esther's body as if pricing it by the pound, 'but yer seems to 'ave put weight on since the last time I saw yer.'

'That's because I'm eating more regularly,' Esther assured her.

Poll jerked her head in the direction of the still open door. 'Does yer new fancy man treat yer right?'

'He's not my fancy man,' Esther bridled. 'He's sort of my adopted father and he's very good to me. I live here now, as you probably know already, if it's one of your associates who's been following me for the past few weeks. That's how you tracked me down to here, isn't it? Well, now you've found me, what do you really want?'

'Don't know what yer on about by suggestin' that I bin followin' yer,' Poll stared her out, 'but I were wonderin' if yer ready ter join me team o' young ladies what can earn easy money on their backs of an evenin'. The way yer lookin' now, I reckon yer could pull in over a quid a night, chargin' up ter five bob a time.'

'I'm not interested,' Esther replied haughtily.

'You'll find me in the White 'Art some time after seven this evenin',' Poll advised her as if she hadn't heard.

Esther raised her voice as she turned to go. 'The traffic noise must be heavier than I allowed for, so I'll say it again, louder this time. I'm not the slightest bit interested in joining your prostitutes' club, so I'll bid you good morning.'

'Seven o'clock in the White 'Art,' Poll insisted.

'I just told you, I'm not interested,' Esther reminded her.

Poll smiled. 'But yer are interested ter 'ear 'ow yer friend Martha come ter die, ain't yer? Seven o'clock in the White 'Art. The snug. An' come on yer own this time.'

Esther made her way back inside Rosen's, her head reeling, while across the road, half hidden behind a stack of railway sleepers in the entrance to the timber yard, Jack felt a heavy hand on his shoulder.

'Caught you at long last. Your mother will be pleased!'

'Uncle Percy! What on earth are you doing here?'

'I'd like to be able to say that I was tracking you down at the request of a sister-in-law who's going out of her mind with apprehension for the welfare of her only son, but in reality I was following Pearly Poll.'

'Why?'

'Before I disclose that piece of confidential information to someone who's no longer authorised to receive it, please confirm that you were spying on Esther.'

'Why else would I spend every day staring at the front wall of a Jewish tailor's shop?'

'No reason other than unrequited passion?'

'What other reason could there be?'

'Do you come here every day?'

'Yes, including Saturdays and Sundays, why?'

'Is that the first time you've ever seen Pearly Poll here?'

'Yes, but why are you following her?'

'My itchy nose. You probably read that the latest Ripper victim was Mary Kelly?'

'Yes indeed — it must have been the same woman we heard about when we were following up on the murder of Catherine Eddowes, right?'

'Only too right — and I was the one who probably led Pearly Poll to her, so that she could send in her tame knife man. The problem — for you — is that it was Esther who got me her address.'

'So you went ahead with that insane plan of yours, despite my protests?'

'I'm afraid so. Now, despite what Abberline and Reid may think, I'm even more convinced that Poll's behind at least this latest killing and probably the earlier ones. They were all women who could point the finger at her.'

'So now she's found her way to Esther, shouldn't we do something to warn her?'

'Forgive me for saying this — and if you're going to throw a punch at me, make it my right side, since I have loose teeth on the left — but I have to eliminate the possibility that Esther is somehow assisting Pearly Poll, perhaps out of fear or something, so we can't warn her that we're on to Poll just yet.'

'Always the policeman,' Jack muttered, 'while the woman I love's become the next target of Poll's crazy knife maniac.'

'You definitely won't like to hear this,' Percy replied, 'but if she is lined up as a target and we keep a few paces behind her everywhere she goes, she could be the means by which we catch the Ripper.'

'You're dead right,' Jack stared in disbelief, 'I didn't want to hear it and I'll do everything I can to stop it.'

'Delighted to hear it,' Percy smiled back, 'since I was counting on that. But we'll have to box clever, since you're no longer on the force. How have you been living, just out of curiosity and so that I can assure your mother that you've not been selling your body in some male brothel?'

'I had some savings,' Jack explained. 'With heavy emphasis on the "had". I'm just about stony now, so it'll be back to Barking for a short while when the rent money runs out this week.'

'I can lend you enough to keep you there while you're helping me trap the Ripper and then we can work out what I can say to persuade Reid to take you back on the force.'

'I was thinking of maybe getting a job in the fish market,' Jack explained. 'I've always enjoyed fishing.'

Percy burst out laughing. 'My brother was right all those years ago when he predicted that you wouldn't be fit to be let out once you came of age. Have you ever seen the inside of a fish market?'

'Once — at Southend.'

'Well, I once had occasion to investigate a knifing at Billingsgate and the main problem I had was that everyone in there had a knife and hated everyone else. Believe it or not, you'll be safer back in uniform.'

'But not for what you have in mind with Pearly Poll?'

'Obviously not. Leave Poll to me to follow, while you stay within hero distance of Esther at all times.'

'Poll knows what you look like, surely, the same as she does me?'

'Of course, which is why I've sent for Detective Constable Atkins, the Yard's best impersonator of a newspaper boy. Some of those you employed on that stake-out in George Yard can also be drafted in on a shift basis and I won't need you, unless Esther crosses Poll's path again. Just so you know, I'll also be armed with a pistol.'

'And to think that Mother always feels reassured when I'm in your company,' Jack grinned. 'It looks as if my stay in this wood yard will be longer than I originally anticipated — any chance of a meat pie and a cup of tea?'

'Consider this your most important lesson in undercover policing,' Percy grinned back. 'There are no lavatory breaks and the catering's abysmal.'

Across the road, Esther was considering her options. She was now safely installed in comfortable accommodation with a substitute father, she had more money coming in than she'd ever contemplated in her wildest dreams and yet she was now seriously considering meeting with a dangerous woman who might be able to summon up a maniac who enjoyed carving women to pieces. Then she remembered Martha, the woman who'd shown her friendship when she was a lonely and fearful young seamstress who was too scared even to go down into the communal kitchen to make herself a cup of tea until the lady across the landing had all but dragged her down there and introduced her to several fellow residents as 'My good friend Esther, what's able ter read an' write, if any of yers needs anythin' like that.'

Whatever the danger, she owed it to Martha to find out how she'd come to die and who had been responsible. Assuming that she survived until the following morning and could avoid being fed to one of Pearly Poll's sexual customers like the sacrificial virgins she'd learned about in Testament classes with Rabbi Goodmann, she could pass the information on to Inspector Reid. Perhaps Jack would get to hear of the assistance she'd been able to render and think more worthily of her. *Don't even build your hopes up there, girl,* said another voice in her head. *Just find out for Martha's sake.*

Telling Isaac that she was going out for an hour to visit a friend from her days in George Street, she slipped out of the rear door of Rosens' in the half light and dodged behind a stationary bus as its driver waited to turn left into Commercial Street. No point in drawing attention to herself, she reasoned, and if Poll had been telling the truth when she denied having her followed, then Esther still needed to do her best to elude whoever was following her, for whatever reason.

As a result, Jack almost missed her. But as luck would have it, he happened to glance down Commercial Street, where he could see someone disappearing into the gathering dusk with that distinctive skipping gait that he remembered so fondly, wearing what looked like Esther's best 'walking out' coat of trimmed fake brown fur. Was it her or not? He had an important choice to make very quickly — if it was her, he needed to follow her, but if it wasn't, he'd be abandoning his post and exposing Esther to potential danger.

There was only one way to resolve the issue and without giving any thought to what he would say if he'd mistaken some other woman for Esther he dashed across Lamb Street, dodging wagons and buses and earning curses from a couple of their drivers. He hammered on the front door of the tailor's premises and an aggrieved looking Isaac came to the door and stared out at him.

'Why would you be requiring alterations after six in the evening?' Isaac enquired.

'I have an important message for Miss Jacobs,' Jack advised him.

Isaac shrugged his shoulders. 'Then I have an important message for you, whoever you may be. She has gone out for an hour.'

'Did she say where?'

'Only that it was a friend where she used to live. Now I come to look at that jacket of yours, it could do with being taken in. Our terms are reasonable ...'

But he was talking to himself, since Jack had shot off like a greyhound, running as hard as he could down Commercial Street in the direction of George Street.

Esther slipped apprehensively into the snug bar of the White Hart to find that Poll was already installed at a table with two other women of dubious appearance and she nodded towards Poll before taking a seat at a table near the far door. Poll left her seat and walked over with a broad smile.

'Mild, weren't it?'

'Yes please — a small one,' Esther replied.

Poll took the opportunity to order herself a large gin and brought both drinks to the table with another encouraging smile as she sat across from Esther.

'Now then, yer friend Martha.'

'Yes?' Esther enquired nervously.

'You think I got 'er killed, don't yer? That's why yer so scared o' me.'

'I'm not scared of you,' Esther insisted unconvincingly.

'Well, I didn't,' Poll insisted. 'It were one o' the guardsmen.'

'At two o'clock in the morning?' Esther reminded her. 'According to the landlord of this place, Martha went off with that guardsman well before midnight.'

'No she didn't,' Poll assured her. 'She were wi' another o' the women — Clara — what were all set ter do the business wi' the guardsman.'

'But ...' Esther began to protest, before Poll raised her hand.

'Shut up an' listen. The arrangement were that Clara an' 'er guardsman would go inter that room on the first floor — the one outside where Martha's body finished up — an' while they was at it, Martha were gonna creep inter the room an' rob the bloke. That worked fine, then it were the turn of another guardsman what were lined up wi' another o' me girls, Mary. Same routine an' another nice little earner. An' on it went, four or five o' them, an' each time Martha were able ter rob the bloke while 'e were at it wi' one o' me girls, 'til we got ter Polly. Then Martha musta got careless, or else Polly 'adn't got 'is full attention or sumfin, but this guardsman rumbled what were goin' on an' chased Martha onter the landin' an' done 'er in wi' this big knife 'e were carryin'. Then 'e ran off smartish an' we was left wi' Martha's body on the landin'. We didn't want it ter look like an army bloke 'ad done it, so I took a knife o' me own an' added a few extra 'oles in 'er body, then we left 'er for some poor sod ter find later.'

Esther was beginning to feel the effects of the beer as she tried to focus on the questions that were swirling around her brain, but which she couldn't quite find the words for.

'The woman — the Polly — that one who ... guardsman ... Bucks Lane ...'

She couldn't quite hear what she was saying because the background noise in the snug had become much louder and was beginning to echo around in her head. She wanted to ask Poll to get her friends to talk more quietly, but she couldn't quite focus on the woman's face. Then it seemed as if Poll was swirling her head around in circles and someone was moving the walls of the room like the horses on a fairground roundabout. Not content with that, they lifted the floor and Esther could feel herself falling into a deep empty canyon.

Jack learned from an irate Sadie Thompson that Esther had not been seen at her former lodgings for some time and as he stood anxiously on the pavement in George Street, his next choice was the best he could have made, given what was happening further south. Instead of retracing his steps and continuing down Commercial Street, he ran into Osbourn Street and headed for Leman Street, intent on making urgent enquiries of his Uncle Percy regarding the current whereabouts of Pearly Poll.

This took him along Whitechapel High Street and past the White Hart, outside which he was intercepted and bundled into a doorway by the very man he'd been looking for.

'You took your time,' Percy complained. 'Your quarry went in there twenty minutes or so ago.'

'Esther's in there?' Jack enquired breathlessly. 'What the Hell for?'

'She's met up with Pearly Poll, which is what I'm doing here,' Percy advised him. 'How come you were running like the hounds of Hell were after you and why the delay?'

'Long story,' Jack wheezed as he doubled over in search of additional breath. 'But how do you know that Esther's in there with Poll? You didn't reveal yourself, I hope?'

'Of course not,' Percy grinned triumphantly. 'Constable Atkins wanders in there every so often, selling newspapers and your former colleague Preedy's doing his drunk impersonations in the alleyway up the side. So we've got them covered from both sides. Here comes Atkins with his latest progress report.'

A youth who looked to be no more than fifteen years old came strolling over with a bundle of evening editions over his arm, a jaunty cap on his head but a frown on his face.

'Well?' Percy enquired.

'They're not in there any more,' Atkins advised them. 'They must have gone out through the other door.

Jack raced into George Yard via the side alley and skidded to a halt in front of the prostrate form of Albert Preedy. 'Did you see Poll come of the White Hart in the company of another woman?'

'Certainly did,' Albert confirmed. 'There were three o' them, actually. Poll and a second woman who looked like a tottie and they were carryin' a drunk woman between 'em. Poll's still inside the doss house, but the second woman came out just before you turned up and went back inter the White 'Art through that side door.

'The third woman,' Jack asked breathlessly, 'the drunk one — how was she dressed?'

'Some sorta cheap brown coat covered in what looked like dead cats, why?'

'And they went into the doss house?'

'Yeah, but ... '

'Give me your billy staff,' Jack demanded.

'You're not on the force any more,' Preedy objected. 'I can't surrender ... '

'Give it me — now!'

Esther began to come round to discover that Polly was even heavier than she looked and was sitting on her stomach.

'You can't kill me in here,' Esther protested. 'They'll connect my body with you when they find it.'

'Yer reckon?' Poll grinned. 'Yer forgettin' that this place is rented be a military gent. That guardsman that everyone reckons did all them killin's'

'You arranged all those killings, didn't you?' Esther said accusingly.

'Whatever yer says,' Poll leered back as she reached down behind her and produced the largest knife Esther had ever seen, even in the hands of the *shochet* butcher from whom her parents used to get their supplies. She screamed and Poll laughed.

'Scream all yer like, sweet'eart. Most folks in this place just minds their own business. They'll find you in 'ere like they found Mary Kelly — another blabbermouth just like you. Pity, you bein' so lovely an' all. D'yer wanna know why the others 'ad ter go, just like you're goin' to?'

'If it stops you using that knife on me, then tell me,' Esther croaked.

Poll smiled and it somehow seemed more threatening than the knife in her hand.

'Well, let's see now. There was Polly Nichols, o' course — she were first. She were there when yer friend Martha got 'er one way ticket an' she were gettin' nervous when the Peelers showed up at the inquest on yer friend. She were dead easy, since she 'ad nowhere ter go that night an' I just follered 'er until we got to a quiet street in a poxy slum area.'

'Then you called in the knifeman, or was he with you all the time?'

'What knifeman? Annie Chapman were next, 'cos she knew all about the little services I were doin' fer pregnant totties an' suchlike in 'ere an' she wanted money ter keep 'er gob shut. So I shut it for 'er, in a manner o' speakin' an' most of 'er guts finished up on display. That's when yer stupid p'lice friends got ter thinkin' that some sort o' loony doctor were responsible. I done Mary Kelly even better, in case she remembered where she went fer the op — thanks fer leadin' me ter that one, by the way.'

'But you weren't the one using the knife, were you?' Esther persisted, playing for time, although perhaps she was merely delaying the inevitable. Either way she didn't want the sensation of that knife entering her soft flesh.

'Why d'yer think it weren't me?' Poll leered back at her. 'In my line o' business, yer gets ter know where all the girly bits is positioned an' it's nice ter play around wi' 'em. That's summat I learned as I went along.'

'But the one who died outside the club in Berner Street?' Esther enquired, desperate in case the conversation was about to end and the slashings to begin.

'Nowt ter do wi' me,' Poll insisted. 'An' the same night I were doin' a little job on Cathy Eddowes, what brought me most o' me customers fer bubby removals. Only she were that sozzled on the drink that it were only a matter o' time afore she went ter the police. The night she finished up inside the pokey in Bishopsgate I reckoned she'd finally done it, but I mighta bin wrong there. An' that's the lot.'

'Mary Kelly?' Esther enquired in a desperate attempt at a delaying action.

'I already told yer about 'er. An' yer've run out o' time, 'cos now it's your turn.'

She held the knife firmly in her right hand as she eyed Esther's throat. Esther tried to scream again, but her throat seized up just as she became aware of an almost forgotten face over Poll's shoulder and heard the heavy 'thunk' of wood on skull. Poll's eyes glazed over and she fell sideways onto the floor, where Jack hit her twice more across the head before looking up at Esther, still lying flat out on the bed.

'You all right?' he enquired.

'Yes,' Esther replied, struggling to sit up.

Jack had a worried frown on his face as he stood up from where he had been examining Poll's prostrate form. 'I reckon I may have killed her,' he confessed. 'That's going to take some explaining.'

Jack walked over to a wardrobe that had its doors half open. Hanging from various pegs were a variety of men's coats and army uniforms, while a selection of deerstalker hats and sailor's caps lay on the shelf above them. They found false moustaches and beards in a paper bag and something horribly smelly and squishy wrapped in newspaper. Jack whistled softly and began reading several half-written notes that fell from the shelf.

'I think we found not only the person who was writing to the newspapers, but also the guardsman, the sailor and every man described by the witnesses as accosting the victims shortly before they died. She must have used one of these disguises when paying the rent on this place.'

Albert Preedy pushed his head round the door and looked down gloomily at Poll's body on the floor.

'Sergeant Enright won't be very pleased,' he advised them. 'We were supposed to be following 'er, not layin' 'er out cold.'

'Go down and bring the sergeant up here immediately,' Jack instructed him.

'You're not police,' Preedy objected. 'And there's the little matter of me billy club what yer stole.'

'Just do it,' Jack insisted and Preedy shrugged his shoulders and wandered out. Jack looked at Esther. 'Are you sure you're all right?' he enquired.

'Perfectly,' she insisted, doing her best to suppress the shivering now that the delayed shock had set in. 'How did you know which room?' she enquired as the thought struck her.

'You have a very distinctive scream,' Jack grinned back at her as he nodded towards the wardrobe. 'Looks like we've saved a few other women who might have been on her list as well.'

'Just because you saved my life, Jack Enright, don't think that we're back to where we were,' Esther insisted. 'But in the circumstances, you're entitled to one kiss, so make it a good one.'

They were still locked together as Percy Enright arrived in the doorway and coughed politely. Jack broke the embrace and stepped back with another of his trademark grins. 'May I introduce you to Jack the Ripper? Take a look inside that wardrobe.'

Percy did as instructed and whistled softly as he took in the implications. 'Her?' he enquired as he nodded towards Poll's prostrate form.

'Her indeed,' Jack confirmed. 'But if you were thinking of hauling her in for questioning, I feel obliged to advise you that I think I killed her.'

'In that case, Jackson Albert Enright, I arrest you on suspicion of murdering a murderer. Take him into custody please, Constable Preedy.'

'You're joking, of course,' Jack began to protest with a look of pure amusement on his face until he realised that he wasn't and turned to Esther. 'Tell him, Esther — I did it to save your life.'

'You'll be required as a witness in due course,' Percy advised her with a sly wink.

'Of course,' Esther replied, 'but right now I have a business to run.'

Chapter Twenty-Three

Esther awoke the next morning to a light tap on her open bedroom door and turned to see Isaac's worried face in the doorway.

'While it is always nice to have visitors,' he remarked, 'it is perhaps better if they do not arrive at your door in a police wagon. It is not good for business and I trust that you have not been transgressing the laws of this nation, *tochter*?'

'Police? Here for me?' Esther enquired sleepily. 'Please tell them to wait outside while I dress.'

'First you must have some breakfast,' Isaac replied. 'If they are intending to place you in a cell, it would be better to have food inside you.'

'Just a cup of tea please, *foter*. I'm not hungry anyway and the longer that police wagon's out there, the worse for the reputation of the business. You don't want people thinking that you've been forging suits.'

He chuckled and wandered back downstairs. Ten minutes later Esther presented herself at the front door of Rosen's and smiled at the uniformed constable with the reins of the horse in his hands. 'I take it that I'm not under arrest?'

'Certainly not, miss. I have instructions to convey you to Leman Street. You must be very important to somebody.'

'That'll make a nice change,' she joked as she opened the side door and stepped in. A distant clock somewhere was chiming nine as she announced her arrival at the front desk in Leman Street and was escorted up to the second level, down the inevitable long corridor and into a room that was already somewhat overcrowded. The man with the black handlebar moustache invited her to take a seat and seemed to be in charge.

'I'm Inspector Frederick Abberline of Scotland Yard and I believe that you already know my Sergeant, Percy Enright, and Inspector Edmund Reid of the local Division.'

'That's correct,' Esther confirmed, just as a constable appeared in the open doorway loaded down with tea and muffins. As he placed them down deferentially on the table between them, Esther was reminded of a young parlour maid in Barking called Alice and wondered why Jack wasn't in the assembled company.

'First of all, my congratulations on your part in putting an end to the worst set of murders that the East End of London's ever suffered,' Abberline smiled as he reached across to the tea things. 'How do you take your tea and would you like a muffin?'

'Milk and one, please, and no,' Esther replied with a smile. 'As for catching the Ripper, I'd be dead now if it weren't for Constable Enright. He was the one who caught her, strictly speaking.'

'Unfortunately he was only a civilian when he did that,' Reid advised her, 'and so we need to take certain steps to cover ourselves in that direction.'

Esther raised both eyebrows at Percy Enright, who simply smiled back at her reassuringly, but remained silent.

Abberline coughed loudly and Reid muttered his apology for interrupting. Then Abberline continued where he'd left off. 'Regardless of how Mary Connolly, to give her correct name, came to be apprehended, it most certainly does seem as if she was responsible for the recent spate of horrible mutilations that came to be associated with the name "Jack the Ripper". In the wardrobe in her room we found disguises to fit the descriptions we had of all the "men" seen with the victims shortly before their deaths and her long career as a street prostitute clearly gave her knowledge of all the back alleyways to be found in Whitechapel and Spitalfields. We can safely conclude that she also knew how to approach women of the same calling and each of the victims was in possession of information that could have led to her exposure, either as a murderer or as an abortionist.'

'What about the so-called medical knowledge?' Esther enquired meekly, before apologising with her eyes for having interrupted what had begun to sound like a public address by Abberline. Fortunately he seemed to be in the mood for explanations.

'She was once a midwife and then she turned her hand to abortion. There are various ways of procuring abortions, which we need not go into in detail, but there can be little doubt that she learned much about the internal layout of the female body during her previous activities, lawful or otherwise. We can only surmise that she coupled this with a strange fetish for anatomy. Enough to account for the injuries on the corpses of her victims, anyway.

'I am led to believe that she drugged you before taking you into the room where you were found?' Abberline enquired of Esther, who nodded.

'I think she put something in my drink,' she explained.

'Probably a strong sedative of the type she employed on her abortion clients,' Abberline explained, 'but if you experience any untoward symptoms in the next few days, let Inspector Reid know and we'll arrange for the police surgeon to look you over.'

'So Pearly Poll did them all?' Esther enquired.

'Except, we think, the murder of Elizabeth Stride,' Reid explained. 'We're still investigating her last co-habitee, Michael Kidney, over her death. But the others almost certainly.'

'So the newspapers can be told that the streets are safe once again?' Esther enquired proudly. It fell deathly quiet and everyone turned to look at Abberline.

'That's partly why we asked you to meet with us this morning,' Abberline explained. 'For various political reasons that I'm not at liberty to disclose, we cannot, at this time, disclose what we know, although we can be certain that there will be no more murders — of that type anyway.'

'I'm afraid I don't understand,' Esther replied. 'Surely it's a matter of considerable pride to the police to have caught the maniac and the public need to be reassured?'

'It wasn't the police who "caught the maniac", as you put it, Miss Jacobs,' Abberline explained. 'It was a couple of civilians — yourself and former police constable Enright — and the culprit turned out to be a woman, despite all our previous assertions that it was a man with medical knowledge. And Mary Connolly wasn't "caught" — she was killed, by an unauthorised civilian, while two Scotland Yard undercover officers and a constable from H Division, looked on from outside the building.'

'But the public?' Esther continued to insist, at which point Abberline's face hardened.

'The public must not be informed, Miss Jacobs. That's why we had you brought here this morning, to secure your undertaking that you will say not a word to anyone about what happened.'

'But how will you explain Pearly Poll's death?' she demanded, scarcely able to believe what she was hearing.

'All that will be disclosed to the newspapers is that a woman was discovered by police officers running an illegal abortion operation from her residence in George Yard Buildings and that she unfortunately died when the lover of her "client" at the time attempted to intervene and was obliged to knock her senseless when she threatened him with a knife. Simple self-defence, no further questions asked, and no charges laid.'

'So Jack will be released?' she enquired.

'If by "Jack" you mean Mr Jackson Enright, then yes, he will — provided that you go along with the version of events that I just outlined.'

'But that will involve me admitting to requiring an abortion, which will bring my chastity into disrepute.'

'Your desire to preserve your reputation is admirable, Miss Jacobs,' Abberline assured her, 'but it will only be necessary should the police be called upon to explain the circumstances of Miss Connolly's death. That in turn will only be required if anyone — yourself included — suggests any other explanation for that death.'

'Isn't that called blackmail?' she demanded, red in the face.

It went quiet again, until Percy Enright muttered, 'No, it's called "police politics", but it will result in Jack's release.'

'Where is he at present?' Esther enquired.

'In a cell four floors down,' Reid advised her. 'We couldn't risk releasing him until we had your undertaking of silence.'

'So you're buying my silence with his release?'

'Basically, yes.'

'And no-one will be any the wiser that you've caught "Jack the Ripper"?'

'No, but at least we know that the killings are at an end,' Abberline reminded her. 'Our primary duty is to protect the public, not tell them how clever we are.'

Esther thought long and hard and the silence was becoming unbearable, before she raised her eyes to look at Percy Enright. 'I don't have a choice, do I?'

'I'm afraid not,' Percy replied, 'but the family will be forever in your debt.'

A tear was forming in her eyes as she looked across the desk at Abberline. 'You have my undertaking to remain completely silent about what happened yesterday evening, but you should know that Jack Enright displayed great courage in saving my life, for which I shall always be indebted to him. But that doesn't mean that I want to see him again,' she added with a sidelong look at Percy Enright.

Chapter Twenty-Four

'There are more flowers in your accounts department,' Isaac advised her one afternoon several months after the death of Pearly Poll. 'I have put them with the others and you will no doubt regard them as being of no account, as you did with all the others. But the man who is sending them — and the note is from the same person as before, who calls himself Jack — that man must hold you in very high esteem. Are you going to break my heart soon and tell your old *foter* that you will be marrying and moving to a new place?'

'You need have no fear of that, *foter* Isaac.' She smiled back at him from the sink where she was washing the lunch dishes. 'Jack and I were once very close, but he thought of me only as a poor girl seeking a way out of Spitalfields and I could not allow our relationship to continue in those circumstances.'

'And you loved this young man?'

'I still do, in my memory and my heart. But it has been some months now since I saw him and who knows how I would feel if we were to meet again?'

'And yet every young girl needs to find a young man who will make her his *kale* — his partner for life. Soon I will be gone and what will you do for companionship?'

'You have many years left, *foter*, so don't speak like that,' Esther frowned. 'But when you are gone, I will also need to find another living and then what?'

'Perhaps I will leave you this business as your *nadn, tochter.*'

'Forgive me, I am not as Jewish as I should be,' Esther chuckled. 'What is "nadn"?'

'The *goyim*, they call it a dowry and I have no-one else to leave all this to. Without you, I would have had nothing anyway.'

'Don't talk in that way,' she insisted with a slight shudder, 'because without you I will have no one.'

'Except this young suitor with the flower business,' Isaac joked as he went back to his sewing machine.

The New Year came and went, but the flowers never ceased arriving, every week and sometimes twice a week. They always had romantic notes attached to them and Esther couldn't help wondering how Jack could afford them all and indeed what he was doing for a living these days. In saving her life he had ruined any chance of resuming his police career and Esther could not recall him ever expressing a wish to follow any other trade or profession. Then one day that question was answered for her.

She was head down over the weekly balance late one Friday afternoon when Isaac answered the hammering on the front door with his usual: 'It is the *Schabes* tomorrow and this evening we close early for prayers at the synagogue. I can see you on Monday.'

'By then these flowers will have wilted,' a familiar voice insisted and Esther rose to her feet with a smile and walked through the curtain.

'Percy!' she exclaimed as she walked swiftly towards him, embraced him and kissed him on the cheek. 'Have they finally thrown you out of Scotland Yard and have you opened a florist's business? And is Jack your best customer?'

'That's three questions all in one,' he reminded her, 'and I'll need to moisten my throat before I can answer them all.'

'Come through the back and I'll make us a cup of tea.'

'This brings back memories of the kitchen in George Street,' she commented as she laid the milk and sugar in front of his mug of freshly brewed tea.

'Happy memories?' Percy enquired with a challenging smile.

'Of course, but ... well, you know.'

'I'm not sure I do know,' Percy replied, 'but these will be the last flowers you'll ever be receiving from Jack, so I took it upon myself to deliver them in person.'

'Has he got someone else?' Esther enquired as her heart sank to stomach level.

'How would you feel if he has?'

'I ... I don't ... oh, please tell me he hasn't!'

'He hasn't, but hold onto that feeling of utter panic and despair that you just experienced if the two of you ever meet up again.'

'That's not likely, is it? What's he doing for a living these days?'

'What he always did — policing, but in a better environment for a promising young detective.'

'I thought he'd resigned before we caught Pearly Poll.'

'So he did, but I persuaded Abberline to take him back.'

'How on earth did you manage that?' she enquired. 'Reid seemed determined.'

'Reid was, but Abberline was persuaded.'

'How?'

'The price of your silence was Jack's release, was it not? Well the price of my silence was his reinstatement to the Metropolitan Police, but at Scotland Yard, where he now works with me. As I pointed out, he'd landed them Jack the Ripper and they'd need to keep him under police discipline if they wanted to ensure his silence as well as mine.'

'That was very cheeky of you,' Esther chuckled, glad to learn of Jack realising his ambition to be a detective.

'Not half as cheeky as insisting that he be reinstated with arrears of pay. After all, he'd spent several weeks following you around to ensure your safety and was there when he was needed to save your life.'

'Are you telling me that once he'd resigned, Jack was the one following me everywhere, not too subtly on occasions? And it was for my safety?'

Percy reached out and took her hand in his. 'Have you the remotest idea how much Jack loves you, Esther?'

'I think I'm beginning to get the idea.'

'And you still love him, obviously.'

Her face began to crumple in impending tears and Percy reached out to hold her tightly as they broke loose.

'I love him so much I want to die some days!' she wailed into his shoulder as he stroked her back reassuringly. 'But how can I admit it and not look like a gutter whore on the make?'

'This place,' Percy enquired as he looked around him, 'is it the one that you worked from in the days when you took in sewing?'

'Yes — it's my "sort of uncle's" business.'

'The old man who was insisting on me waiting until Monday?'

'Yes — Uncle Isaac.'

'I don't see anyone else around — are you his business partner?'

'No — only his employee, but only just recently he was talking about leaving the business to me one day.'

'So you're an heiress?' Percy suggested.

'An heiress to a very modest business, yes, but so what?'

'Hardly a poor seamstress living in lodgings,' Percy observed.

'I've certainly come on to that extent, yes,' Esther conceded.

'If Jack — a humble police constable — were to propose marriage to you, some people would liken him to an adventurer after an heiress's fortune, would they not? Or have I been reading too many novels by Jane Austen?'

'I couldn't think of Jack like that,' Esther objected.

'Then what makes you suppose that Jack thinks of you in those terms? Did he say anything like that?'

'No, but ... well ...'

'His mother?'

'Yes. But if she's thinking that, she must have got the idea from Jack, mustn't she?'

'Him, or Jane Austen,' he grinned. 'I once told Jack that I needed to bang your two heads together. Now I think what I need to do is to sit the two of you down together in the same room and act like the referee at a prize fight.'

'I'm not sure what I'd be able to say to him, after all this time,' Esther mumbled as she wiped her nose now that the tears had stopped.

'That's why you need the referee,' Percy assured her. 'Anyway, thank you for the tea and now I'd better be getting back. Jack and I are trying to catch burglars in Chelsea at the moment, so we're working nights, since that's when burglars work.'

Isaac stepped smartly back from behind the door at which he'd been listening to their conversation and went in search of pen and paper.

'There is a letter for you this morning,' Isaac advised her as she came downstairs and into the kitchen. 'It has been posted from Barking, or so my tired old eyes tell me — who do you know in Barking?'

'A family I used to visit,' Esther replied absentmindedly as she read the return name and address on the back of the envelope. *I wonder why Lucy would be writing to me, but I think I can guess who gave her the address,* she mused as she tore the rear flap of the envelope and read the short note.

My dear Esther,

I do hope I may address you by your first name? Pardon my presumption, but I shall be journeying into the City next Wednesday and was wondering if I might leave two or three gowns for you to alter in your new business premises? I was so impressed with your work on my blue gown on the occasion of your visit here and unfortunately I am still growing, although not in height.

I anticipate being there at around two in the afternoon. If this is not convenient, please write or telegraph me before then.

Kindest regards,

Lucy Enright

'More business, *foter*,' Esther assured Isaac as she left the kitchen and headed for her work space behind the curtain. 'A quality customer this time — the sister of that young man who could afford to send me all those flowers.'

'This is good,' Isaac replied. 'But you should charge her at a discount if you wish to acquire regular business from such a customer. The wealthy, they are always seeking discounts — which is perhaps why they are wealthy.'

Wednesday finally dawned and Esther took considerable care with her dress, even though she would be doing her normal day's work; at two o'clock she had an appointment with a very important new client, one to whom he had formed a natural attachment during their only previous meeting and one who could bring much custom to their business. Shortly after lunch, Isaac answered the knock on the front door and Esther stepped from behind her curtain to renew her acquaintance with the beautiful and now even more elegant, young lady who was holding out several long gowns in a carrying bag.

'Esther,' Lucy beamed as she kissed her on the cheek, 'it's been too long, and I have put on far too much weight in attending other peoples' weddings with my new fiancée, Edward Wilston the architect. We are to be married in June, but my bosom seems to have swollen with so much pride that each of these gowns needs to be altered to accommodate it.'

Esther smiled reassuringly. 'One deft action with my tape measure and your problem will be solved.'

'I don't care how much it costs, if you can perform your magic. They are my best gowns and the only ones I dare be seen wearing in decent company.'

'I'll give you a special discount,' Esther offered, remembering Isaac's instruction. She picked up her tape measure and ran it round Lucy's upper torso, noting a few measurements down on her notepad.

'When do you require them?' she asked.

'There's no hurry,' Lucy assured her. 'I come into town every Wednesday, since my fiancé has his offices in Holborn. He's taking me out to supper this evening, but this means that I have a few hours to kill. Would it be possible for us to take a healthy walk somewhere?'

'This is Spitalfields,' Esther reminded her with a smile. 'You no doubt smelt the far from fresh air as you came down here and there's enough horse dung in the streets to pave the district three times over.'

'Jack told me of a churchyard where you and he used to walk in happier times,' Lucy recalled. 'Perhaps there?'

Esther had some urgent work to finish, but Lucy promised to be a valuable customer, so she willingly agreed and collected her coat and gloves, then escorted Lucy through the bustling thoroughfares to Christchurch yard and the familiar gravestones that brought back such happy memories.

'How is Jack?' Esther enquired as casually as she could, but even so in a voice that wavered slightly.

'I wouldn't know,' Lucy replied, 'since we don't see him any more often now that he's with Scotland Yard than we did in the old days. Do you miss him? I know he misses you.'

'So Percy implied, when I saw him a little while ago.'

They were approaching the centre of the old grave section, where huge stone sarcophagi marked the final resting place of various local worthies from the days when Spitalfields was synonymous with easy wealth and ten foot high crosses surmounted with angels and Biblical scrolls pointed up into the sky.

'I must own that I'm feeling a little parched,' Lucy complained. 'Did I see a lemonade stall as we came in?'

'Yes indeed,' Esther confirmed, 'it seems to have always been there.'

'I'll just dart back and get some,' Lucy offered. 'Would you like one yourself?'

'Yes please,' Esher smiled and watched as Lucy stepped carefully over the uneven grass in her fashion boots. It brought back memories of her first Sunday with Jack, when they sat on the bench just inside the gate and she insisted that he hold her hand. A hand she would dearly love to hold again.

'Make that three,' came a voice she had never dared hope to hear again and as she turned with a jolting heart, Jack stepped out from behind one of the tall tombstones. He had never looked so apprehensive and she had never seen him look so beautiful.

'Oh God,' she whispered.

'You can call me Jack, if you promise to hold my hand again,' he grinned and she almost lost her footing as she rushed forward, threw herself at him and burst into floods of tears.

'Please, please forgive me!' she pleaded as she finally stopped kissing him, allowing his lips to resume their normal shape.

'Forgive you for what, precisely?'

'For treating you so horribly, not acknowledging all those beautiful flowers ...'

'I'll forgive you if you marry me,' he beamed and Esther immediately placed two fingers over his lips as an admonition to silence.

'Don't spoil it so soon,' she whispered. 'Just hold me tightly, kiss me and promise me that we'll go walking again every Sunday.'

'Yes, ma'am,' he murmured as their lips locked yet again.

'You might need these to cool you down,' came a voice from behind them, as Lucy stood a few paces away, beaming happily and holding three bottles of lemonade.

Chapter Twenty-Five

Lucy left them in order to go shopping 'up West' and Esther gleefully took Jack back to meet Isaac, who shook him warmly by the hand, congratulated him on his choice of flowers and quietly whispered in his ear, while Esther was making the tea and happily humming to herself, that if Jack did anything to mar Esther's happiness, he would be 'cursed like only an old Hebrew like me can curse.'

'Don't worry, Mr Rosen,' Jack assured him, 'all I want is to persuade her to marry me. How may I best achieve that?'

'By loving her, reassuring her and holding her hand in bad times. That's what worked for me, anyway.'

The next few Sundays were spent renewing their acquaintance with the churchyard that had become their Paradise and Jack tactfully avoided the topic of marriage, content that they were back holding hands, kissing and exchanging mutual assurances of their love for each other.

'So how is life at Scotland Yard?' Esther asked him one Sunday. Jack's beaming reply left her in no doubt that at least one part of his life was fulfilled.

'Very exciting, always different and sometimes dangerous. An escaping burglar took a pot-shot at me a few nights ago. He missed me, but winged one of my colleagues, who's now in Charing Cross Hospital fighting for his life. If he dies, the bloke we caught will swing for it.'

Esther shuddered. 'I'm sorry I asked. There's no risk of you being shot, is there?'

'Not if I keep my head down. Most burglars only have clubs and knives anyway.'

'Let's talk about more pleasant matters,' Esther grimaced. 'How are the arrangements progressing for Lucy's wedding?'

'Fine, so far as I know. We're invited, by the way.'

'Obviously you're invited,' Esther acknowledged, 'since you're the brother of the bride. But me?'

'The sweetheart of the brother of the bride,' Jack smiled. 'And Mother insisted.'

'Probably only to balance the numbers at the table afterwards,' she suggested.

Jack stopped for a moment, gathered her in his arms and reassured her: 'Please don't go back to demeaning yourself again, Esther. That's how we parted last time — you wouldn't want that, would you?'

'No more than I'd part with my right hand, which is my best sewing hand,' Esther smiled as she kissed him.

'I think that was a compliment,' Jack said as he kissed her back.

May was turning into June and the wedding was only a fortnight away, when Esther came downstairs one Friday morning to find the kitchen empty. Isaac was normally the first up and would put the pot on the stove for the first tea of the day before making an early start at his sewing machine, so when he wasn't in the kitchen Esther went into the main work room. When he wasn't there either, she tiptoed up two flights of stairs and found him lying on the floor at the side of his bed, white as a ghost and not breathing.

She raced downstairs and out into the street, wide-eyed and trembling in shock. There was a policeman on point duty at the junction of Hanbury Street and Commercial Street and he directed her to the nearest physician, Dr. Mellowes of Bishopgate Street. The doctor collected his bag and escorted

Esther back home, where he examined Isaac briefly, before advising Esther that Isaac had probably been dead for several hours and that it had likely been a seizure.

Esther quickly learned all there was to learn about engaging undertakers, organising funerals and coping with silence in a rambling old building that had once been an audience to the old man's wavering renditions of folk songs from his youth as he worked away happily at the latest suit, or stirred the pot for yet another of his delicious and very filling, *kosher* dishes. Much of that advice came from Jack when she broke the sad news to him the following Sunday and it was he who suggested that they go through the old man's papers. In an old floor safe they found the will, dated only a few months previously, leaving everything to Esther.

'So now you're a woman of substance,' Jack smiled. 'You know what I'm going to ask you next, don't you?'

'Please don't Jack — not yet, anyway,' Esther begged him. 'Just tell me that you know how to make suits, or else the business will have to close.'

'Can't you employ someone for that?' Jack enquired.

Esther shook her head. 'I'm really not ready to become an employer, Jack.'

'Even if you're not,' Jack reminded her, 'the building must be worth almost a thousand pounds on its own. It's three stories high, on a main road and in the best part of Spitalfields — that is, as far away from Whitechapel as possible.'

'I'm already feeling uncomfortable here on my own, Jack. The floorboards creak at night and when the wind's blowing there's something on the top floor that rattles and I can almost imagine that it's old Isaac working on his sewing machine.'

'Don't tempt me to ask the forbidden question,' Jack grinned.

She smiled back. 'I'm not afraid of ghosts, as far as I know, but I am afraid of committing to something that may not be right. Can't we just stay the way we are?'

'Probably not,' Jack replied quietly. 'Not if the sensations I get every time we even touch are anything to go by.'

'I'm glad I'm not the only one,' she sighed as she held him to her, 'but let's just wait a little longer. I don't want to have to seek out the services of another Pearly Poll.'

'I owe you both my thanks and a heartfelt apology,' Constance Enright admitted to Esther as they stood together on the rear lawn of the house in Church Lane, drinking yet more champagne as they relaxed after the wedding ceremony and the meal that had followed, excellently prepared and served by outside caterers. They had just waved off the happy couple as they took the coach to the station, ahead of catching the Boat Train to their honeymoon destination.

'I'll start with the thanks,' Esther replied in a voice slightly slurred by her third glass that day.

'Thanks for making Jack so happy again,' Constance replied, no more sober than Esther. 'According to Percy, the poor boy was like a three-legged puppy until you took him back into your affections.'

'He was never out of them,' Esther reassured her, 'but what is the apology for?'

Constance hesitated for a moment, then got it off her chest at long last. 'I may have given you the wrong impression that day when I enquired after your life to that point. I didn't think for one moment that you were after Jack for his relative wealth, although Heaven knows there won't be too much left of that if I keep on enjoying rude health like this and eating into the family trust that my late husband established. It was unforgiveable of me to create the impression that I was of the opinion that you were "on the make", to put it in vulgar terms.'

'I was more concerned about what Jack might think,' Esther explained. 'I thought that you might have got the idea from him.'

'Not once — ever,' Constance reassured her. 'He was furious when he learned what I'd said to you and I would have bitten my own tongue out if it would have made any difference. Anyway, you're now back together again, so when can we expect another wedding?'

'We're almost on the point of talking about that,' Esther advised her, smiling.

'Make it soon, then.' Constance smiled back.

Several weeks later the old building in Lamb Street was placed on the market and Jack took a few days off from his police duties to assist Esther in the tiresome business of showing potential purchasers around the premises. Several of them sniffed in disapproval at the remains of the former business that Esther had somehow never got around to removing, since they reminded her of the second father figure that she'd lost and on long afternoons she could sit quietly at Isaac's old sewing machine and tell him in teary whispers how much she owed to him, how good he and Ruth had been to her and how much she hoped that he could hear her in Heaven.

Other potential purchasers quibbled about the number of bedrooms, the adequacy of the internal plumbing, the ongoing need for the privy in the back yard and the state of the roof slates, but eventually an offer of seven hundred and fifty pounds came in and Esther accepted it, before realising with a start that this made her homeless once the long entry date of October 1st came round. Then, late one afternoon while they sat discussing her options, there was a heavy knocking on the front door and Jack went to answer it. He came back with a serious looking Percy, who lost no time in stating his business.

'There's been another slashing in Whitechapel, two nights ago. The inquest's already under way and I've just come from the first day's hearing. Reid's on tomorrow and he wants you two down there to hear what he's going to tell the coroner, so that you all get your stories right.'

'So we didn't get the real Ripper?' Esther enquired, open-mouthed.

'You probably did,' Percy assured her, 'but Reid's preparing to bluff his way through this latest one, without giving too much away. If I can stay here the night, we can all go down there tomorrow.'

The latest victim was yet another ageing prostitute, a woman called Alice Mackenzie whose body had been found in a virtual blind alley off Wentworth Street, her head almost hidden underneath a scavenger's wagon, with her throat cut and several other deep wounds on her body reminiscent of the horrors of the previous year. Two police surgeons — Dr Phillips and Dr Bond — disagreed over any similarity between this murder and those inflicted by the Ripper and it now fell to Edmund Reid, who'd been called out to view the body when it had first been discovered, to hose down any suggestion that the Ripper had struck again, without disclosing the true reason for his confidence.

Jack and Esther sat holding hands in the fourth row back from the front as Coroner Wynne Baxter plodded his way through the type of inquest with which he had become all too familiar. He called Edmund Reid to the witness seat and enquired as to what connections, if any, there were between this killing and 'the ones that so darkened our East End streets last year'.

Reid cleared his throat, opened the paper in his hand, lifted his head to be clearly heard and announced, 'With the authority of the Commissioner for the Metropolitan Police, I can assert with every confidence that the death of Alice Mackenzie was brought about by the hand of a common murderer and not the sexual maniac who gave himself the name "Jack the Ripper". We will, of course, leave no stone unturned to bring this new killer to justice, but we believe their motive to have been an entirely personal one between the victim and their killer and not the work of the deranged lunatic who we confidently believe to no longer be in our midst.'

'How can you be so certain?' Baxter enquired.

'Twenty odd years of police experience,' Reid replied, 'which has made me more familiar with the mind of the criminal offender than the average person. The reign of terror by the person calling himself Jack the Ripper is at an end, but extra manpower has been drafted into the area, to give renewed assurance to the people of Whitechapel and Spitalfields that they may go about their daily lives in safety — unless they are unfortunates who constantly court danger from their perverted customers in dark alleyways. Thank you, Mr Coroner.'

Baxter announced another adjournment until a new day to be fixed and Jack and Esther wandered outside.

'Let's hope that's an end to it,' Esther murmured as she took Jack's arm.

'Certainly,' Jack replied as he reached into his pocket and extracted a small padded box covered in purple felt, 'but we have one matter left to resolve.'

'Not here, Jack,' Esther pleaded as she became acutely aware of the passing pedestrians, in whose constantly moving flow they were a stationary island.

'Yes here, Esther,' Jack insisted as he took the ring from the box. 'Esther Jacobs, will you marry me?'

'Give me one good reason.' Esther half smiled back at him.

'I love you.'

'Another one.'

'You have the money for a house to set ourselves up in and have babies.'

'Another.'

'You love me.'

She giggled, then burst into tears as she threw her arms around him and hugged him hard. 'Yes.'

'About bloody time,' Percy Enright commented from close behind them. 'Just don't ask me to be the flower girl.'

A NOTE TO THE READER

Dear Reader,

Thank you for taking the time to read this book and I hope that it lived up to your expectations. I've always been fascinated by England's most notorious series of unsolved murders and when I began writing historical fiction, it was a natural choice for me, at the end of my career as a practising criminal lawyer.

I hope that dedicated 'Ripperologists' will take into account that this is first and foremost a work of fiction, although I took considerable care to weave my story around the known facts regarding the 'canonical' series of atrocities. I also acknowledge that not everyone ascribes the first of these — the murder of Martha Tabram — to the Ripper, but perhaps that is why the possibility was overlooked, both at the time and by subsequent armchair investigators, that the person responsible for those that followed might have been covering up their involvement in the first of them.

Having given literary birth to my two main characters, Esther and Jack, I found them impossible to leave teetering on the brink of matrimony, and there are three sequel stories scheduled to be published by **Sapere Books**, in which Mr and Mrs Enright combine their talents to unmask other perpetrators of dark deeds.

I've been writing novels for most of my adult life, but have only just got around to having them published. As a 'new' writer, I would therefore welcome any feedback and support that you, the reader, can supply. You can, of course, write a review on **Amazon** or **Goodreads** or you can contact me online via my Facebook page: **DavidFieldAuthor**. I'm more than happy to respond to observations, reviews, questions, or anything else that occurs to you, or to join in any 'thread' that you care to begin.

I look forward to getting to know you better online.

David

davidfieldauthor.com

Sapere Books is an exciting new publisher of brilliant fiction and popular history.

To find out more about our latest releases and our monthly bargain books visit our website:
saperebooks.com